FAST FORWARD

⟩⟩

Published by FF>> Press.

ISBN 13: 978-0-9817852-5-7
ISBN 10: 0-9817852-5-5

Library of Congress Control Number: 2011929571

cover art: Chris Henry (hellochrishenry.com)
cover design: Stacy Walsh
typesetting/layout design: M.D'Alessandro

FAST FORWARD PRESS

FAST FORWARD PRESS

≫
PRESENTS

THE INCREDIBLE SHRINKING STORY
a collection of flash fiction
volume 4

EDITED BY
kona morris
leah rogin-roper
& stacy walsh

FF≫ Press 2011

CONTENTS

INTRODUCTION
flash fiction: the art of concision

Having been an editor for the Fast Forward flash fiction anthology for the past four years, people often want me to answer the question, "What is flash fiction?" Sure, short stories have been around for centuries, but the official genre dubbed "flash fiction" is still new enough that many people want a definition.

The simplest answer is just that it is a very short story. How short depends on who you ask—some publications consider flash fiction to be any story under 2,000 words, others say 200. At Fast Forward Press, we use 1,000 as our word limit. Why? Because we had to stop somewhere.

But here's the catch: It needs to be authentically short. It is not a brief summary of a longer story, or a hasty reflection of a character's entire life. Flash fiction is meant to begin and end within a couple pages; it is not a long story crammed into a tiny form like a grown woman trying to squeeze into her four year old's tutu and pass herself off as a child ballerina. Brevity has nothing to do with the story's purpose, it just happens to be the common trait of this genre.

After considering the word count, it's really just a matter of how good the story is at engaging its readers. Like a little ant carrying something fifty times its size, the strength of a flash story must be able to stand up against any length piece. And the best ones can make you feel like you have experienced as much plot, character, meaning, and mystery as found in an entire novel, in a mere page.

To successfully create more meaning than would intuitively be thought possible in such a short space, flash fiction often relies on the tools of ambiguity and implication to create engagement in its readers. The words the author chooses not to write are equally as important as those they use.

One of my favorite flash pieces is Raymond Carver's story, "Popular Mechanics" (from *What We Talk About When We Talk About Love*), where he gives no background, shows an intense moment, and then ends it in a terrifyingly ambiguous way. As readers, we have no choice but to be left in a state of enthrallment because we are haunted by all the things we don't know—all the possible outcomes that our brains involuntarily, morbidly fantasize about.

Ernest Hemingway's famous six-worder, "For sale: baby shoes, never used," is an excellent example of the power of implication. In this piece, he gives just enough information to force us to imagine a back-story. Most people immediately assume that something tragic has happened, even though nothing has been made explicit—it is merely implied by the set up of a situation that feels off; our brains do all the work.

I choose pieces for our anthologies that are memorable to me, that have, in no more than a few minutes, ingrained themselves into my mind. The greatest flash fiction stories are the ones that you can't even remember the length of because the only thing that matters is how much of an impact they had on you.

And that brings me to our latest collection of 59 stories, all of which I am thrilled to be presenting. As you read through these pages, you will find that the stories are arranged from the longest to the shortest. We have designed the collection this way in order to bring attention to how they maintain strength even though each one uses fewer words than the one before it. If you flip through the pages, you will see the length of the text physically shrink—thus our title: *The Incredible Shrinking Story*.

Our collection begins with Rob Geisen's 1,000 word story, "The Night I Discovered That I'm Not as Cool as Han Solo," which is a perfect way to show how a consistently strong narrative voice can carry the momentum of a piece. When I originally read it, it didn't occur to me that it was the longest story in the collection because the energy is so potent throughout.

Following in the footsteps of Hemingway, Michael Flatt's six-word story, "Seven Cock-rings Later," ends our anthology with exquisite precision. Flatt employs the full capacity of implication by giving information that is counter-intuitive and forcing his readers to ponder in what possible universe this scenario could actually exist. I love the way it is a story because it *implies* a story, with a choose-your-own-adventure style of freedom for readers to imagine the background for this very bizarre reality.

The moment a story gets us to think, it has won. This is why implication and ambiguity are often the greatest tools a writer of flash fiction has to inspire their reader's imagination beyond the mere walls of the word count. Engagement is the ultimate goal of any piece of writing, and flash fiction just has to make it happen a whole lot quicker. It is in this way that it has set itself apart from other literary genres, and it is for this reason that it has made an art form out of concision.

Now, please come inside the world of flash fiction, where stories are much larger than they appear, and allow us to take you on a fantastic journey across the impossibly vast pages of *The Incredible Shrinking Story*.

Cheers to you and to the infinite number of
outcomes of twenty-six letters,
-Kona Morris, February 2011

THE NIGHT I DISCOVERED THAT I'M NOT AS COOL AS HAN SOLO

rob geisen

We all know that scene. The one from *The Empire Strikes Back*, on Cloud City, after the gang's been betrayed by Billy Dee Williams. Han Solo's stripped of his black Han Solo vest, and while standing there in front of everybody in a nice white shirt and brand new handcuffs, seconds away from being frozen in carbonite and shipped off to Jabba The Hut, Princess Leia lays it all out there and tells Han, "I love you."

And like Keith Richards or something, Han Solo says, "I know." All cool and shit. It's one of my fondest memories from childhood. I'd always aspired to handle myself like that, if circumstances ever presented themselves. Which they did. Sort of. In the form of Helen.

We shared a very similar moment together. Only instead of saying, "I love you," she told me she was leaving. And instead of me taking it like a multi-galactic rock star, I broke down sobbing, mumbling in the midst of this breakdown something that sort of sounded like, "Please don't go!"

It wasn't a pretty sight. As the fog kicked in and I felt myself being slowly lowered further and further down into the carbonite pit, I became even more desperate at the thought of never seeing Helen again. I started screaming stuff like: "Are you sure you want to end this? I mean, I can do better! This is crazy! Will you at least read to me while I'm frozen? That would be nice. And while you're thinking it over can you get me a sweater or something?! It's cold in here! That'd be great, darlin. I need you!"

Helen nixed the idea with a silent head shrug that meant, 'No.' I continued haggling desperately like a pre-frostbite riddled buffoon.

"Do me a favor!" I scream as the pit slowly overtakes me and I can no longer feel my own genitals. "Don't fuck Lando! Can you at least promise me that? I mean, he's a friend of mine! It's the least you could do, in honor of my love for you! Keep your stuff away from his dick!"

I hear Helen say she can't promise anything. It's an embarrassing scene. The last thing I hear is Boba Fett making fun of me and Chewbacca gargling something about how he's lost all respect for me and refuses to be my sidekick anymore, insists on hanging out with someone more 'manly.' He's currently on tour working as Justin Bieber's sidekick instead.

And just like that, it's over. Or maybe it begins again. My life inside this pit.

While frozen in carbonite waiting for my love to not rescue me, I find a strip mall bar and order several drinks. While waiting for them to arrive, I flip off Storm Troopers and stare at the coked out alien who has a face that looks like something that fell out of an elephant's vagina nine months after Jack Nicholson fucked it. His nose hanging loosely like a Skeet Ulrich sized dick.

I sip my drinks quickly, trying to forget where it is I really am. Frozen in carbonite. Vest-less. Publicly rejected and doomed.

Over the course of one long goddamned scene, I've managed to get dumped by the only girl I've ever loved. I've lost my sidekick to an un-pubed pop star, not to mention the respect of the entire Bounty Hunter community. My girl's probably blowing the only black friend I've got in this entire galaxy, and because I've seen how these sort of movies end, when I finally do get out of this carbonite outhouse, I'll have to spend the next several years attempting to get over her, which, in this nightmare, manifests itself in the form of being trapped in the Redwood Forest over the course of a ridiculously disappointing sequel battling armies of Gary Coleman sized teddy bears while the dude who's fucking Helen steals my ship and blows up a second Death Star!

I ask you, where is the honor in that? How is this fair?

And then I realize I'm being an idiot for even asking the question.

Belief in fairness leads to trusting. Trusting leads to leaving your goddamn apartment. Leaving your apartment leads to meeting the woman of your dreams. Meeting her leads to having drinks together. Drinking together leads to huge boner sex. Huge boner sex leads to a scary couple of days waiting to find out if you maybe have herpes (after the fact, she mentions that she might have herpes). Maybe having herpes leads to not having herpes (hooray!). Not having herpes leads to love.

And we all know where it goes from there. Love leads to suspicion (why the fuck does she have to smell like Colt 45 all the time?). Suspicion leads to betrayal (because she was already secretly having butt sex with Billy Dee Williams, that's why). And as we've already covered, Billy Dee leads to public humiliation and getting frozen in carbonite. Which leads to drinking alone with all the other aliens in this bar. Which eventually has led to me accepting free shots from an Irish dude who talks like Yoda and insists everything's going to be fine. Which leads to, I don't know. I don't care if Yoda can levitate an entire bowl of cashews without spilling any nuts. Yoda not spilling his nuts all over everything fails to convince me that I'll get over her soon and things will be okay.

It's at this point that Yoda gives up on his pep talk and starts showing me tiny holographic images of AT-ATs having sex. Photos of AT-ATs going at it robot doggie style leads to me paying my tab as my brittle nerves jump to light speed.

I miss you, Helen. I'm sorry I'm not as cool as Han Solo.

I'm still frozen without you. It's all this goddamn carbonite, damn it.

I don't know how to let you go.

COVERING THE MOON

myra king

In the distance we hear a noise like tapping. I stop some feet short of the entrance to the graveyard, my brother Ben snuggled up on my back, his head buried in my parka hood.

"Look Ben," I say, "it's not the dead you have to be scared of."

Our mother tells us this all the time. We live close to the cemetery, actually only a glance away through our front door. Not that we knew instinctively to be frightened, but our friends soon let us know that it wasn't a normal thing. Aren't you afraid the ghosts will get you? How can you sleep? Stuff like that. But it's not the dead that do bad things. It's the living. Like Dad, he left us soon after Ben was born. And Ben, well, he was a rape baby. Everyone knows this, even Ben, although he doesn't know what it means. And even though everyone always says, "Poor Mrs. Anderson," that's our mother, I always think, *Poor Ben*. It's a lot worse for him.

Yeah, the dead can't hurt you, but that doesn't stop us from being scared.

We have done this: visit the graveyard at midnight on every Friday the 13th since Ben turned three. It was a dare set up by my friend Anica. After the first time, she chickened out, but we kept it up like a tradition. This is our fourth year. I'm eleven now and Ben is seven, but it's a good thing he's such a scrawny kid, he doesn't weigh much. I guess the rapist must have been a small guy 'cause our mother is nearly five foot eleven and built like a rugby player. Sometimes I wonder how he managed it. There's this Australian spider called an Orb-weaver. The female is so much bigger than the male that he has to be very careful when mating. I think maybe the rapist would've had to be careful with Mum. I've seen her temper and how hard she uses the strap, especially on Ben, when she's been drinking. But maybe the rapist had a knife or a gun. Mum's never told me the details, and you can't ask about things like that, can you? I mean, I'm not supposed to know, but my cousin Daniela heard her mum, my aunty, telling a neighbour. Daniela told me and then Ben heard me telling Anica. But none of us have told Mum we know.

The tapping noise is getting louder. It sounds like someone with high heels, but the paths are all gravel and sand so that can't be right. I don't know if it's coming closer to us, or if we are moving closer to it. The dare is to reach the middle where the little buildings are. The mini-mansions, I call them. They glow sort of in the night, but I can't see that yet, we're still a ways away.

I jump at Ben's voice, muffled by my parka. "I gotta pee, Sis. Now."

I lower him down and he goes behind a bush, even though we can't see anyone and the tapping is still ahead of us.

When he comes out he offers me his hand, which I take with outstretched fingers until I'm sure it's dry. Then we both walk on in silence. The tapping noise seems to be coming from where we are heading. But I still can't see the mini-mansions.

Ben pulls on my hand. "Sis," he says, "what does a rape baby look like?"

My mind can't find the words to answer him straight away. So he tugs at my hand again, almost pulling me sideways.

Up ahead is an angel statue, I've never seen her before, she's sitting in the centre of a huge plot divided into four, two at the front and two at the back. She looks like she's about to take off. For a moment I wish I could fly away, too.

There's an iron seat across the path from her. I lead Ben across to it and sit down. He brushes leaves off the seat. He really is a tidy kid, especially for a boy. I have no idea where we are. Which way is home.

I'm gathering my thoughts like someone rounding up sparrows. They keep scattering.

"Well, Ben," I say, "a rape baby isn't the baby's fault. It's still a baby, like any other."

I can feel Ben's eyes on me, staring, and when a cloud passes and the moon and stars light up his face, I see he's been crying.

"Oh, Ben, you're not *that* scared are you?"

Ben shakes his head and looks at the angel. "It's just that Jack said rape is a bad thing and that I was a bad thing, and that's why Mum hates me. And I was wondering, Sis, will I go to hell?"

I can't answer him this time. The trouble is I don't know exactly how rape works. I know Jack is right, it's something bad and I know that it's something to do with mating. And also the girl doesn't want it.

But does that mean the roosters are raping the hens? I see that all the time, the hens running away and the roosters jumping on them and pushing them into the dust. The hens certainly don't want it. The baby chickens are cute though.

Ben is sucking his thumb and leaning against me. Me and him against the odds.

I realise I can't hear the tapping anymore and I wonder when it actually stopped, how I missed the moment. I look around, back the way we came, and at the way I think we should be going. I don't know if I can find the strength to carry Ben much further.

The clouds are covering the moon again. I didn't think it was possible to get lost in a place we are both so familiar with. But everything looks so different in the dark.

BELIEF

curtis smith

The ping pong ball bounces over the tightly packed glasses. Mesmerizing, the bony echoes, the ball's erratic dance. The center's red glass earns a prize from the coveted top shelf. There must be a plausible strategy, some twist in one's release, but you have yet to grasp the connection. You hand the next child three more balls.

Watch the ball. The baby inside you kicks. Tap your stomach's curve, and the baby kicks again. It's a game you play, a call and response that eases your loneliness.

Stringed lights hang from the rafters, electric starshine for the base's rec hall. Christmas carols play over the crackling PA. The children tumble across inflated castles. Echoes, a hundred echoes. A few larger figures wade amid the throng, parents in camos, the base commander in his dress blues. Stooping, the adults chase and tickle—a tribe of loving giants.

"Who's next?" calls Maureen, your table partner. Reindeer antlers bob atop her head. She is nearly old enough to be your mother, and you are thankful she is here, her cheer and enthusiasm making your gaming table one of the more popular stops. Earlier, she stepped outside to call her teenage children, and you felt lost without her, your voice barely a scratch against the din.

Two corporals burst through the doors. The music stops, and on the sudden breeze, you smell the sea. The soldiers stride forward, their chests thrust. "Attention!" barks one of the soldiers, and both corporals jerk into stiff salutes. The castles' inflating motors purr, but the bouncing has stopped. The doors open again. A collective gasp greets Santa's entrance.

Their motors cut, the castles melt into plastic puddles. A charge fills the air, a palpable current of hope and dreamed-of reunion. Santa makes his rounds, the dumbstruck and giddy believers by his side, the tentative in an outer orbit. The base commander and Santa exchange salutes.

Maureen slips on her coat. "Mission accomplished," she says. The noncoms are already taking down the other tables. Outside, a damp chill on your skin, but far from the winter cold of home. Gaze to the sky and think of your husband beneath the same stars, half a world away.

"Sure," you say when Maureen suggests a ride into town. You have nothing waiting but a quiet apartment and a book you're not sure you want to finish. Rust circles the wheel wells of Maureen's car, but the interior is clean. At the gate, she jokes with the sentry about a red-suited intruder.

A deeper darkness waits outside the razor-wire fence. The road is flat, sand on the shoulder. In the brush, the orange eyes flash then disappear. Crack your window. The salty air sinks into your lungs. Maureen says this will be the third Christmas in the last four years without her husband.

You hit town, a main drag of strip malls and supermarkets, and in the older parts, churches and bars. Soldiers on every street. A boy on a bike darts in front of you. Maureen fiddles with the radio until she finds Christmas music. The reindeer antlers remain upon her head. She reaches beneath her seat and produces a pint bottle. Light glimmers in the brown liquid. "Do you mind?" she asks.

You drive to the suburbs where Maureen wants to show you a neighborhood known for its Christmas light displays. Here, the streets wind in gentle curves, the houses set far back from the curb. Maureen parks along the end of a cul-de-sac. She pulls a long drink from the bottle. A silhouette passes across a bay window.

And the displays are beautiful. Trees wrapped in white, illuminated branches reaching to the sky. Wax bags line the sidewalks, a candle burning in each. The shine against the darkness makes the houses seem weightless, like they are a breath away from breaking free of the earth and returning to their rightful place among the stars.

Maureen tips the bottle again. You smell the alcohol, harsh and biting. Your baby kicks. On the radio, a song you haven't heard in years. Maureen claims her husband is a good man but naïve. He thinks he's fighting for his country, but here, she says with a sweep of her bottle-holding hand, is who he's really fighting for.

A sip, that's all you want, a taste to forge a communion with this time and this woman. The warmth floods your throat, a shudder down your spine. Before you can hand the bottle back, the police lights flood your car.

You sit on the curb, hands upon your head. The officer holding the breathalyzer studies your belly. You squint when the light is shone into your face. Your arms, still raised, grow heavy. You answer questions, *Yes, sir; no, sir.* You explain you just wanted to get off base and see some Christmas lights. Along the cul-de-sac, forms gather behind their windows, curtains pulled aside then shut.

The officers take the bottle. They threaten you with a night in jail, but instead they allow you to return to base as long as Maureen doesn't drive. Maureen says nothing, but you thank them, once for you and once for her. Slide the seat back to accommodate your girth. The cruiser haunts your rearview until you return to the poor part of town.

Along the main street, Christmas decorations hang from the light poles, candy canes and plastic trees, all of them tattered, survivors of December storms long past. The reindeer antlers rest on the dash. Maureen lays her head against the passenger window. It's only when you turn down the radio that you realize she's crying. You wish you knew what to say, but that part of you is empty tonight. Instead, you sing along with the radio; it's a song you know from childhood, a time you went to church and believed such things.

RESIDUE-TR 6:30-9:20

paul piatkowski

The vibration along the wood of the bar only loosely kept me rooted to the plot. The setting itself, neon glowing from beer signs, a busty bartender leaning across the wood and wiping the counter free of an abandoned bottle's ring of perspiration, stomach-scratching hormone-driving slow wiping, a stench of menthol and tobacco pinching my nostrils in the wake of a one-eyed ogre and a brunette to my right, all effectively stimulating my senses. Self-awareness my goal this evening.

Sliding my eyes away from the surplus bust venturing out from the tightly buttoned blouse, I was able to make an explicit gesture towards my throat, as of a man who is thirsty or dying. The barmaid maneuvered behind the counter, adding a button to help distract my tongue. I noted the possibility therein: conflict or perhaps climax.

"Russian formalism," I squeaked.

Her disillusionment in regards to my manliness was visible. "Stoli okay?" she asked me.

"Sure," I said, wondering how the hell I had just

ordered vodka. It must have been some postmodern trick. I wanted bourbon. Submitting to a primitive urge, I began carving symbols across the wood with my pocketknife.

The barmaid returned with my clear glass of vodka, a lemon limply leaning on its lip, and a nice brown shot, while frowning at my wood-scratched artistry, hating semiotics and the brain pretzels she would have to eat later deciphering my cave drawings.

"B-But—," I stuttered, though I need not have attempted to construct language. She pointed towards the ogre, the man waving his arms emphatically in greeting.

"You started this thing *in medias res*," he shouted over the brunette's teasing and the cacophony of the room. "Better get a move on with the action or there will be no function to this piece."

I saw the truth of his statement; I had always been a good student. His brunette looked me over, less flat than she had seemed before, and she shifted a little of her weight against my thigh. Heat rose to my cheeks and, lingering for a pause (or were those two words just two ways of saying the same thing?), tucked the shot back. She smiled and her palm hovered above mine for a moment, the center of all my creative attention on the pouting pudginess of her lips.

I walked on back to the crowd, hearing the bartender and that one-eyed ogre popping beer bottles behind me: pick, pack, pock, puck, the caps flipping into trashcan, onto counter, ground and floor.

The rhythm followed me, sweat misting me and limbs clipping me, at times a thigh on a detour against mine, weight falling down my stomach and settling heavily in my crotch. I could feel the heat of the inferno. Breaking through the pack, I finally reached my seat. The vodka was more than half empty. Two friends I had arrived with were sitting and discussing Levi-Strauss and Derrida.

"Didn't he just write a cookbook or something?" the chubbier of my two friends asked. He scratched at his poorly balanced beard.

"Well," my spectacled friend responded, "I suppose if we are willing to submit to the idea it is a cookbook, then it is a cookbook. Signs are signs."

"Stop being so contrary," the other responded, blowing air into his cheek to make the beard appear more full after noting my observing him—I could never maintain a good enough distance for indirect characterization.

"Arbitrary, you mean?"

"Ar/bitrary?"

"Don't de-center my argument with your slashes."

Just too heady for me. The light show on stage was really amazing and my head slowed down a little in the circles it had been running. I turned down the jay they tried to hand to me, though I inhaled the secondhand smoke to make it clear I was no prude. I desperately wanted to clarify my virility despite my previous claims of being above any of that—too serious about my work to worry about audience perception. Perhaps I had built my identity upon a false supposition.

Noise still itched at my ears (merging the senses for imagery sake) and I wandered closer to the band to get a better perspective. Bodies swarmed around me, my shirt sweaty, sticking to my chest, and my headband was moist. The music had turned psychedelic and the absurdity of the gestures did not escape me, though I was working hard again in order to find the meaning in it.

The band, The Paranoids (straight out of a Pynchon novel), were in the middle of a song that sounded a great deal like "Rocky Raccoon," though imitation. The line between fiction and reality blurred and I found myself hearing gunfire when the shots went off in the song: pick, pack, pock, puck.

Suddenly, a storybook blonde appeared out of nowhere and stole the spotlight. Her black bra was well defined through her sweat-drenched white top. Her long fingers were soft, and when she squeezed my shoulder during a nearly "Day Tripper" song, scenes of fantasy projected in my mind. I felt animalistic. A sudden pounding in my crotch made me look around at the band to see if the reverberations began there or in my own body. She planted her lips on my neck and whispered to me.

"You seem like you know who you are. Let's go and fornicate."

I had to laugh at the irony—I had no idea who I was, after all, though every line delivered declared more and more identity, theoretically.

As I walked away from the bar, the one-eyed ogre waved at me.

"Nice job! *Deus ex machina* to close it off!"

I smiled at the eye-patched Joyce and made my way to my iconic, bad-ass Cadillac and drove off with the girl into a full moon that swallowed us whole.

THREE DAYS

nathanael bryant

My first book had just been published. That morning I received a couple of emails from some fans who had loved my short stories and said, "Thanks for the novel." *Immortal Solitude*, based on my marriage, and the first novel of many. One can hope, right? I had not even seen the book on the shelves yet. That's why I was confused when this woman, this Janet Reed, showed up at my door. I had removed my information from the listings before moving into this house. My ex-wife didn't even have my new address, and I intended to keep it that way as long as possible. She took everything else, she wasn't getting my privacy. The only reason my agent knew where I lived was because he helped me move in. And this Janet Reed, so called, had known it was my house. It wasn't some neighbor who thought they had recognized me while I was moving in or anything like that. My agent has no sense of humor or I might have thought he was playing a joke.

She had said she knew me, but I didn't know her. Clearly. I would remember someone that creepy. She smelled of old person, had brown, rotting teeth, and everything about her made my spine crawl up into my brainstem and scream, "Witch!" So I lied and told her my name was John Updike, not Richard Vallary. Why Updike? I couldn't think of another name fast enough, and I had been reading *Rabbit, Run.*

"Well," she persisted, "Mr. Updike, I would like to give you this." She handed me a small envelope, the kind that holds cards with bouquets. "And when you decide to be Mr. Vallary again, read it."

I tried to be nice until she turned to leave, but my "Witch!" screaming brainstem overpowered my higher functions and I slammed the door in her face. I turned my back and leaned against the door, tried to calm my breathing, slow my heart, and stared at the envelope. My name was written on it in tidy, Lilliputian handwriting. I pulled it closer to my face. Under my name were the words, *c/o John Updike.*

In my mind, I had dropped the card and slid down the door, but really my hands were tearing open the envelope. Inside was a small white card; it read, *Three days…*

I flipped the card over to see if there was any more information, thinking, "Is day one today or tomorrow?" The back side had one word: *Today.*

I really did drop it this time. And I ran into the bathroom, my bladder screaming.

Day 1: What do you do with this information? Three days 'til what? I thought it best to confirm that my will was in order. Then I made a list of all the things I had not done, but wanted to.

—See Mt. St. Helens

—Hunt a lion

—~~Write a book~~

—Sing an impressive rendition of "Don't Stop Believin'" at karaoke

—Becky Monroe, my high-school crush

—Streak

Then I found a bookstore and stared at my book on the shelf for about two hours. No one bought it.

Day 2: I marked one item off my list. ~~Streak~~.

I called my mother and told her I loved her very much and thanks for putting up with my whiny, moody, egotistical, artsy-fartsiness in college.

Ate three pints of Ben and Jerry's: Chubby Hubby, Dublin Mudslide, and Phish Food, my absolute favorite. Then added Go to Ireland to my list. Then vomited.

Finished the final chapter in my sophomore work, so they'd have something to release posthumously. Those are always fun for the fans, of which three wrote emails this morning. I wrote them back, wondering if they would each claim to be the last person to speak with me.

I tried calling Becky Monroe. It took me two hours and seven phone calls to random old school acquaintances to find out where she was living and her phone number.

I had to leave a message.

I made sure to sound calm and cool and could we meet up for coffee for old time's sake?

Day 3: I didn't really want to get out of bed, even when I heard the tow truck outside beeping and rumbling. I don't know why, facing the end of my life, I was still worried about losing my car. I got up slowly, used the bathroom, put on a robe, and walked out the front door. I'm sure my hair was still a mess.

I'm not really sure what my plan was before I saw her, Janet Reed. She was signing something on a clip board which she handed to the tow truck driver, who immediately climbed into his vehicle of despair and left, my '07 Honda in tow.

Janet saw me and smiled. I'm sure my facial expression was somewhere between drunken idiot and "just-walked-in-on-my-parents" teen.

"Mr. Vallary," she said. Her teeth were gleaming white. She looked so much nicer today. "You are six months late on your car payments and the bank has repossessed it."

"But, I'm..." I tried to work up some spit in my mouth, "not going to die?"

She shook her head.

"You're not a witch?"

"No, sir. Just very good at my job." She smiled again and slid into her car.

My head was spinning and I must have wandered back inside. My phone rang. Its tinny rendition of "The Power of Love" drew me into the kitchen where I found it and mumbled, "Hello?"

"Richard? It's Becky Monroe."

THE ARMENIAN FLYER

devin murphy

Since the Flying Armenian Circus first came to town, I have learned the names of each bar and rope, each aerial apparatus, and I have seen people leaping around the tent tops—becoming birds. I now know the language of their act and have seen static, dance, multiple swinging trapeze artists, popping tricks, swivelling dynamic flips, and all because of that first time when I was eight years old and I sat looking up at 'The Flyer,' the Armenian woman with the white slipper straps coiled around her calf muscles, which rose off her ankle with the subtle curve of a champagne flute.

In the air, the tips of Princess Natalia's toes touched the back of her head. Her butt bubbled up into a convex little muscle. When she was upside down, the arch of her back heaved her chest forward. The dark line of her cleavage was perfectly visible as she flipped above us, each strand of her tightly coiled black hair caught the sheen of the spotlight, which slid down every lock like she was glowing. I felt everything and understood nothing in the stands where I sat with my tiny erection, memorizing every detail of this woman who could fly.

I was lusting and loving for the first time, the most powerful of my life. When the Princess's show was over, the spotlights dropped to the ring announcer on the ground. But I kept my eyes on the dark overhead. I could see her in the shadows as she descended a beam behind the bleachers and snuck out the back of the tent. My younger brother, Connor, and older sister, Jamie, did not notice that I slipped under the bleachers from my seat and snuck towards where Princess Natalia had exited the tent.

Behind the Big Top there was a line of Airstream caravans bent in a crescent moon from the tent. The caravans were enclosed by a tall makeshift chain link fence. I saw her jog-walk into one. I ducked along the tent so no one would see me and made my way to the back of the caravan. There was a window in the back of her Airstream that had opened slats, but it was too far over my head. The only way I was going to be able to see her was by climbing up the side of the fence, which I did as quietly as I could. The tips of my shoes set into diamond shaped gaps in the fence and my fingers strained at the knuckles from hanging there. When I was high enough up that my shoulder blades were facing the window, I craned my neck to peek through the slats.

The flyer's back was to me when she bent over and shook out her hair. She was humming, but in a way I had never heard that set into my bones and has stayed there. She unclasped something on her blouse, which she pulled off like a cape so the heft of her breasts hung loose. My fingers wrapped tighter around the fence. I had never seen a woman naked before. Her brown right nipple was flush against her skin. I wanted to run my hands over every part of her like she was clay, like I was forming her, and even then, even at eight years old, I felt my insides reaching towards her as if I'd just been flung off a swinging trapeze. Then she bent and uncoiled the strap of her shoes. Her strong and smooth back faced me. She stood up, ran her fingers along the elastic of her leotard pants, bent down and pushed them around her ankles. Her rear end was facing me, and for a moment I thought it was the window slats that were throwing me off. But the slats were horizontal, and as I narrowed my focus on this woman, I saw the most beautiful thing I had ever seen, a flesh-colored length of spine hanging down that wrapped over the crack of her butt like a caulking seal. It was only about an inch and a half thick at the base and it thinned as it sloped down about six inches to a fine rounded point.

Princess Natalia turned sideways to me then. Her tail hung slack and flush from her lower back. She looked towards the slatted window, through the opening, into my eyes, all the way through them to the deep end of my life. At that moment, I let go of the fence and retreated.

That image was in my head the next Monday in school art class. I took pink fleshy colored Play-Doh and formed a tube-like tail by kneading and rolling it back and forth against the table with my hands. When I held it in front of me in my open palms, my classmate, Lenwood Murry, called out so everyone could hear, "This homo made a penis," and the whole class turned and looked at me with this thing in front of me like an offering.

By that time I must have already sensed the oddity

of my desire, and decided 'homo' was a far better word to be called than whatever it was for what I now wanted so badly. So I turned to Lenwood, held out my hands even further, and said, "It's a penis."

NINE THINGS YOU DON'T KNOW ABOUT ME

ann hillesland

1. I make excellent cheesecake.

I've never made a cheesecake in the four years we've been married. But a slice in a restaurant is not the same as eating cheesecake that you've whispered to and coddled to keep from cracking. My cheesecake isn't smothered in cherry pie filling or a slimy sour cream topping. It's light, smooth, with a delicate hint of lemon—my own cheesecake.

2. For the past year and a half I've only pretended to balance our checkbook.

I figure, the bank has got to be better at math than I am.

3. In my twenties my favorite drink was a piña colada.

Sometimes I still get a craving. About six months ago when you were out of town I went to a bar, a place with purple couches shaped like jelly beans, *TinTin* prints on the wall. A young woman with long blonde hair and a short suede skirt flirted with two young men. When I was younger, I never grew my hair out, dyed it blonde or wore miniskirts. I didn't feel I was beautiful enough. But 30 is not too late. The drink smelled like summer, like suntan lotion and cold Fresca and the ocean stretching endlessly.

4. I always speed when I listen to Bruce Springsteen's "Thunder Road" in the car.

I sing along so loud my voice cracks on the high notes. I never sing this way at home, at least not when you're around. But alone in the car, I floor it and speed away.

5. I keep love notes from an old boyfriend hidden in a box in the guest room closet.

When I unfold the crinkled sheets of lined notebook paper I remember studying for our Survey of English Lit class together. We sat next to the creek that ran through our college campus. He read me love poems, and I guessed who wrote them. I remember the wet, secret smell of the creek, the sound of bicycles whirring past, the way his flannel shirt grew warm in the sunshine as I leaned my cheek against it, listening to his chest vibrate with love words.

6. When I was fourteen, I told a secret I shouldn't have.

I told some friends that I had seen my father kissing a woman in front of our house when I was home sick from school. It was autumn. The leaves had thinned enough that looking out of my second-story window I could see my dad in the car with someone who was not my mother. Someone with dark hair and sunglasses pushed over her forehead. After I told my friends, they never looked my father in the eye again. I still had to, but telling the secret meant I couldn't pretend it never happened. Since then, I've been a champion secret keeper.

7. I didn't want you to take the job you have now.

When you asked me, I lied and said it wouldn't bother me if you had to travel so much. I didn't realize how the house would expand without you, how the silence would seep into my bones in the long evenings. How I'd feel when you came back cold with the chill of airports, talking nonstop of hotels and conference rooms, of pulled pork sandwiches and lobster bisque and bratwurst, of people I would never meet and a life grown larger. I didn't realize how much all the little shared day-to-day things weighed when added up over months. How much ballast they gave until they were gone. I hate it every time you pack your suitcase to fly off again, but I never say anything.

8. I know your email password.

First I tried my name, my birthday, our anniversary. Then I tried your first dog's name, which worked. I imagined you in a hotel room, champagne in the plastic ice bucket. The room lights dimmed, and outside the bright skyline of a city distant beyond imagination. A blonde in a red slip. But I only found baby pictures from a co-worker, evites to parties we never went to, and alleged humor from your brother.

9. I almost had an affair last week.

His name is Andrey. He's a programmer from Russia who sits three offices away from me. At first it was just breakroom chat—Can you believe there's never any coffee made? Who put out the stale cookies and why am I eating them?—but then it got personal. How he missed his parents in Russia. How he was scared of the bar scene and had no idea how to meet women. So, three months ago, I started going out with him while you were out of town as his "wingman." I was supposed to draw other women into conversation with him, help him make contact. But somehow the other women never materialized, and we'd end up drinking vodka and talking until last call. I always took off my wedding ring before these evenings, so the other women wouldn't think we were married to each other, I told myself. At the end of the evenings, he'd hug me and kiss me on the cheek. But last week, he slid his lips across my vodka-flushed cheek and to my mouth. I kept kissing him, his lemon aftershave sharp, my heart speeding into the night.

NIGHT DEPOSITORY

meg tuite

Flo met Duane online. After a few multi-dimensional chats about *Columbo* reruns, musical talents, and their favorite hamburger—a consensual preference for Wendy's double with bacon—they decided it was time for a face-to-face.

Duane and Flo met at their local Wendy's and ordered the #2 simultaneously. They nested themselves together almost every night after that in beef, fries, and chocolate malts.

Duane idolized Flo's folds and crevices. He was a bedspread of a man who liked his women loaded.

Things were moving rapidly toward that word "commitment." They spent every evening together watching *Columbo* behind dinner trays of fried foods and towering desserts. When they had their first bout of textbook sex it seemed perfectly natural.

Duane changed his tune after a few weeks of the missionary position and began experimenting. Sometimes he spread hot dogs between her toes and bit on them one by one, or sometimes he'd suck malted pools out of her armpits with a straw. Flo was not averse to food coming into their bed. She liked to feel devoured and kinky in a nourishing kind of way. Things started to get uncomfortable for Flo when the buffet table turned on her, so to speak.

Duane now wanted to be filled with the fodder. Flo found it amusing, at first, to stuff hors d'oeuvres up his ass like sausages and fruit cups. But soon that wasn't enough for his ever-widening pleasures. She was begged to load his cannon with Big Macs, Black Forest cakes and rotisserie chickens, which took some creative packaging on Flo's part. Duane writhed within this unrestrained enema-like ecstasy by night and then careened in and out of offices like a bloated, bow-legged bovine by day. No one but Flo was the wiser.

One night Flo pleaded with Duane. She didn't want to compress his receptacle any longer. He was already lying face down on the bed, pantless and arranged like a pig about to be stuffed, when she arrived. The object next to him unnerved her. She knew that this would be their undoing. She wanted to run, but looking at the back of his spit-shine-reflecting ebony hair and naked flanks, wide as Texas, she couldn't. Duane filled up her life as she was now going to fill up his. She took the object in hand and carefully spread his cheeks.

Flo remained in the ER waiting room after Duane was rushed in, butt up in the gurney. There were bitings of tongues and snickering when Flo explained Duane's dire situation. Flo had suspected that Duane's scatological escapades would overload him.

The doctor and staff were entertained. This was the first time they'd have to extract this particular object from the anal cavity, although they'd seen many objects come their way in the ER. The nurse applied lubricant liberally and the doctor was handed some forceps. He worked up a good sweat for fifteen minutes to no avail. How had Flo lodged this one upright? Duane was given a shot of muscle relaxant and Oxycodone that stopped his whimpering. The object had been sucked in by the sphincter that was now holding it hostage. More lubricant was applied, his rectal jowls were held apart, and the doctor was given longer, more streamlined forceps.

The doctor and staff worked for over an hour. A small incision had to be made to open the cavity wider and finally: success. The doctor pulled out an amazingly intact, unreadable DVD from Duane's rectum. The nurses wiped it clean. They were determined to have the title after all that work to relay a story that would soon travel around the hospital as fast as radio waves.

"Wow," said one nurse. "Never would have guessed a *Columbo* episode would have stimulated so much sexual tension?" The snickering started up again and, as the night progressed, so did the jokes.

Flo felt uneasy driving Duane home in silence. He had to sit on a donut cushion to ease the pain and he'd been given more painkillers to make it through, but the humiliation was all-pervading.

"Well, at least we learned that DVDs only fit into one slot," Flo struggled to smile. Duane gave her a daunting glare. Flo knew it was over.

Duane went back to battling computer idiots. Someone at the office had a wife whose best friend was a nurse who'd been in the ER that night, of course, and so the raucous banter became eternal.

"Hey Duane, whatcha watching tonight?"

"Hey Duane, maybe you oughta get one of those camcorders with the smaller DVDs? Might be just the right fit for a good homespun movie."

"Hey Duane, I've heard *Magnum PI* might be a good ride if you like nestling in with the reruns."

And on and on it went.

Duane and Flo went their separate ways without much fuss. Duane gave up on the chat rooms, stopped eating Wendy's burgers and started going to a gym.

Flo found she couldn't stomach Wendy's or many of the foods she'd once loved. A rotisserie chicken only brought up vivid visions and nausea. She'd lost some weight, as well, by becoming an uncultivated bulimic. Food came up of its own free will.

Flo and Duane would always have one thing in common, though. They would never watch another episode of *Columbo* again.

PRESENTLY TENSE

alec cizak

He wakes up and realizes he's in the midst of a panic attack. He cannot figure out why. He throws the sheets off of his bed and jumps up and paces his room. His heart thunders, beats so fast, so hard, it threatens to knock a hole through his chest. Looking around his room, he realizes that nothing is familiar. There are books on a table near his bed. He picks one up and examines the letters on the spine. "I've forgotten how to read!" He opens his dresser drawers and rummages through clothes he has no recollection of having ever worn. The most disturbing revelation makes its way to the front of all his frantic thoughts and he says it out loud: "I don't know who I am!"

He runs into his bathroom to look into the mirror. The reflection he sees is a total stranger. He tries to remember his childhood. It doesn't exist. Who were his parents? "What did I do last night?" he asks his empty apartment.

He goes through his bedroom and his living room looking for clues. He finds three framed pictures on his kitchen counter. The stranger in the mirror is in every one. There is a picture of him in a black gown worn for graduations. He wonders if it was high school or college. "Are these people beside me my parents?" he asks himself. The next photograph shows him standing with two guys who look similar to him. He assumes they are brothers. "I wish I knew where they were," he thinks, "so I could call them up and maybe they could tell me who I am." In the last picture he has his arm around a lovely brown-haired woman with green eyes. He is smiling in the photograph, she is not.

He realizes he missed something in the bathroom. Something important. He goes back in and scans the floor and the toilet. Nothing seems unusual. The shower curtains are closed. His heart picks up once more as he senses there is someone in the tub. "Hello?" he says. There is no answer. He walks over and yanks the vinyl curtains to the side. He jumps back and holds his mouth.

The woman from the picture, the one who wasn't smiling, lies there, dead. Her throat has been cut. The man drops to the floor. He is barely able to breathe now. "Oh God," he says, over and over. Then he wonders, "Who's God?"

And his world collapses.

He feels the ink on his body, all over. He understands that the apartment and the mirror and the woman in the tub are just like him; they don't really exist. He looks to the sky, or at least, where he thinks the sky should be, and he says, "Dead woman in the tub? Surely you knew something so contrived would give yourself away!"

I realize my character is addressing me. I look around with a 'Who, me?' expression on my face.

The man becomes angry. "Why are you making

me so flat?"

"Excuse me?"

"You put me in the present tense. I have no ability to reflect on anything that's happened in the past. This isn't a story. This is reality television."

I'm barely twenty years old. I can't take criticism from real people. I sure as hell won't take it from a character I created. I straighten my shoulders. "I can write in any tense I choose."

"Not if you want your work to last," says my character.

I fold my arms across my chest in defiance.

"Your prose is ugly, undisciplined."

"I don't remember anyone ever telling me there were rules about which tense you can write in."

"It may not be written down in any of those books third-rate hacks write on writing to tell fifth-rate hacks like yourself how to write the best-seller the third-rate hacks have never quite been able to write, but it's a rule and it's a good one."

I laugh. I think about accusing my character of being addicted to the status quo. Then I remember that I created him and any flaw he might possess is a reflection of me. "Consider me a rebel," I tell him. "I'm breaking that stupid rule."

The character is now calm. He speaks in a mellow tone. "I understand the need to break rules," he says. "Most rules were meant to be broken. This is not one of them."

"Why?"

"Because," says the character, "I'm not comfortable. If your own characters aren't comfortable, imagine what you are doing to your readers. Your opaque, present-tense prose doesn't let them into this world."

I still refuse to listen.

"In that case," my character tells me, "I'm going to stand completely still until you make my existence three-dimensional."

After pretending to really, really think it over, I took the character's advice and rewrote the story from the beginning:

Stanley Croker woke up. He was panicked, though he could not readily figure out why. His sheets were soaked from his own sweat. Looking around his bedroom, he felt something was missing. Then he remembered—Maggie had left him the night before. At least, she told him she was leaving. His heart beat faster as he realized Maggie had never made it out of his apartment.

THREE MONTHS OF RETICENT SILENCE

aisley crosse

He knew it the day she bought the test. He just had this feeling when he saw it there, the bright pink label shining through the grey grocery bag. She was pregnant, wasn't she? It was like expecting the pink slip before getting it; this feeling of dread washed over him and made his stomach quake with nerves. He didn't say anything though. He'd thought to and then she'd seen him looking and asked him to go mow the lawn.

It grew into a physical weight, the knowledge that he was being lied to (made worse by omission!), and despite his unexpressed wishes, she'd stolen his sperm and was making their baby. For the next five weeks he felt used, like a toilet brush in the men's room of a Mexican restaurant. But she smiled and hummed, making herself busy preparing high nutrient salads and booking doctor's appointments, never even stopping to ask him what was wrong.

He waited for her to tell him; he'd have his say then. As the son of a pacifist and a psychologist he wasn't a very confident man—besides, what made him sure he'd seen it in the first place? It could have been tampons—they had pink labels, right?

As weeks continued to pass, her skin took on a new glow. She took pills with her oatmeal and filled the fridge with all-natural, omega-3, whole wheat, bran stuff. And he began to sneak out for chili cheese dogs and ice cream.

It wasn't that he was all together opposed to the thought of children. He didn't mind them when they came over with his sister, or hers. He'd just decided that right now he didn't want any of his own. It was because of his father—a shameless man who'd abandoned his pregnant wife at a full service gas station just west of Colorado in the summer of 1978. She'd gotten out to pee and when she came back, he was gone. Without even twenty-five cents left behind in the dust to use the payphone.

He knew she wanted kids to spite her mother; she'd always said that she was going to be a better mom, a more attentive one who cared about her children and didn't use them as her own personal laundry service. She was going to sing to this child, and read it stories. It didn't matter if it was a girl or a boy; he knew she would love it, just because it was hers.

They'd been pregnant once. Seven months into the relationship she came to him, and they'd fought. She miscarried a week later and blamed him. He blamed himself, too. In her cries, he heard his father's laughter, echoing like nine-year-old boys gathered in the schoolyard shouting, "Fight! Fight! Fight!"

And so she said nothing and he didn't ask. She began to re-organize her study, asking him occasionally for advice on wall colors and throw pillows. She wanted to "cheer the place up." He grunted, shrugged and pointed, well beyond words at this point, then went back to boxing the Christmas lights and paying the bills.

One day, he came home to find a moving van in the driveway. He panicked and ran into the house, shouting her name and thinking she'd left him for good. She laughed when he stopped short at the top of the stairs, almost falling down at the sight of her desk and bookshelves being replaced by a day bed and changing table.

That was the affirmative, the changing table, he despised it and resented its presence. "A gift," she told him, "from your sister. Gabe's too big for it now, and she didn't want to just *throw* it away—it's in perfect condition. Besides," she mused, running her hand along the dark wood rail, "we'll use it. One day."

Slowly, but faster than he'd imagined, his world was sinking in on him. What would she tell him when it came? That it was really a doll? "Oh you know," he imagined her saying, "one of those life like ones they use in the high schools—for when we're ready." She'd nod.

Her stomach was starting to show; she would have to say something soon. What about when the child began to kick and stretch? Wasn't there something he could do?

And then late one afternoon, near the end of the winter months, he came home early. She was in the bath, her head hanging and tears running down into the water. Was it time to ask now? He wondered. Or was it time to go do the taxes? The weeks were slipping by so quickly.

Three days later she came to him, as he'd been hoping she would. He was mentally re-alphabetizing their DVD collection when she crawled into bed, a small smile on her face, and wrapped her arms tight around his chest. Then she pressed up against him, took his hand and laid it on her stomach. For the first time in two months and twenty seven days, he felt something, a small flutter, a sign of the new life awakening between them.

5:19

jason sinclair long

The last time they visited their cousin, Joshua, the twins were three and thus had no memory of the visit, or of him. Now ten, they were more aware of their surroundings and had developed long enough memories to make the events of a weekend stay more indelible. For weeks, the twins had been crushing on their cousin's school photo with his haircut not unlike their favorite rock star. At dinner, Joshua listened to his iPod in one ear while simultaneously carrying on conversations with everyone. Seconds after responding to their mother, his Aunt Clara, Joshua seamlessly lip-synced along with the song in his ear. To Penelope and Clementine, he may as well have been walking on water.

Later that night, after double scoops of chocolate ice cream, the girls gladly gave up *Hannah Montana* and watched Joshua deftly manipulate his Nintendo Wii. "I can stop playing so you guys can watch your show," Joshua offered.

"That's okay," the twins answered in unison.

Joshua kept his eyes on the screen while speaking.

"That's cool, the way you guys talk at the same time."

The girls simply giggled in stereo, Penelope on Joshua's left, Clementine on his right.

Two hours before bedtime, the doorbell rang and additional relatives poured in. One of the adults said, "It's a regular family reunion." The twins were introduced to their great-grandmother, ninety-seven year old Ester. She was friendly enough, but smelled like an old coat. For the rest of the evening, she sat in a large green chair staring at nothing while everyone around her talked and drank wine from a box and ate Hershey's Kisses. The adults said things like, "Well, we all know about Evan's little problem," and, "You wouldn't believe how low Louise has sunk these days."

At bedtime, Penelope and Clementine were thrilled to discover they would be sleeping in Joshua's room. Crossing the threshold into a teenage boy's domain was akin to archaeologists discovering a lost civilization.

"Penny," Clementine whispered, while they brushed their teeth and changed into pajamas in the bathroom.

"Why are you whispering?" Penelope asked.

"He might hear us."

"Oh."

"Anyway, do you think he'll let us call him Josh?"

"Or how about Joshie?" Penelope giggled and then, through her laughter, "Penny, Tiny, and Joshie."

"It's too perfect," Clementine added. "Like a movie or something."

Joshua's room was different than they had

imagined, but somehow exactly what they had expected. Posters covered nearly every available space on the walls, mostly hip bands and snowboarders. The twins swooned, drugged by the kaleidoscope of images. Joshua remarked that just because he'd never been snowboarding (yet), he still felt a "connection to the mountain." The girls thought the way he said it made him sound famous or something.

"You guys can use the bottom bunk," Joshua said flatly and hopped up the wooden ladder to the top. "See you in the morning."

The twins lay side-by-side, breathing in unison, holding hands, not sleeping for hours. Instead, they communicated by squeezing coded messages into one another's hand. It was a secret language they had invented months earlier and serendipitously perfected on the eleven-hour drive the day before. They practiced by commenting on aspects of travel: *Gas stations stink; Dad's singing is bad; Mom's asleep.* Now, lying in Joshua's lower bunk, the girls traded thoughts on everything from his hair to his pants to his enviable Nintendo skills. Eventually, they fell asleep, but only after the messages digressed into sleepy nonsense.

They were simultaneously jerked from sleep by a single sound coming from the hall outside Joshua's bedroom. It was a craggy, demanding voice, saying something about a train.

Penelope was up first because she was on the open side of the bed, but Clementine shadowed her every move. The girls opened the bedroom door, stepped into the hallway.

"Am I late?"

Great-grandma Ester stood before the twins, stark naked, clutching an ancient suitcase in one hand.

"Is this the platform for the 5:19 to Chicago?" she said. "I'm off to see my boyfriend, Willy Stubbs. He's back from the war."

At first the twins didn't realize they were still holding hands but now messaged frantically back and forth.

What should we do?

I don't know.

"Are you two going to Chicago as well?"

She's crazy.

Just old.

"Willy's promised to take me to Wrigley Field to see the Cubs play and buy me a hot dog."

Someone's coming.

Penelope and Clementine watched, seemingly silent, as their uncle Tim turned great-grandma Ester back toward her guest room. He apologized to the twins before sending them back into Joshua's bedroom. They closed the door most of the way and watched through a thin slice as Tim hooked arms with his grandmother. He was very calm and methodical as he walked the old woman down the hall, explaining that the train was delayed and would be arriving after sun up.

The girls lay in bed awake the rest of the night, at first pulsing thoughts back and forth, but eventually running out of things to say.

CHRISTMAS STORY, 1995

peter lindstrom

Santa Claus came to New York City on Sunday night. He got drunk. Santa got drunk sitting next to me at a bar called "The Place." It had a row of booths, a long bar, a jukebox, and an Irish bartender. And me and Santa. We got drunk.

"No one believes in magic anymore," Santa said. "I'm fading."

"Fuck 'em!" I said. "I'm sick of worrying about all the stupid people."

"Without them, I'm no one."

The bartender came over, emptied the ashtray and asked me with a nod if I wanted another drink. I slid my glass toward him.

"You still got that jammin' red suit," I said.

Santa leaned back from the bar to get a better view of himself. He looked over his suit with a tight grin. I lit a cigarette, then the bartender returned with my drink. A rock n' roll song came on the jukebox, a song I liked, and I tapped my fingers on the bar to the beat of the drum. Santa finished his beer.

"Do you want to go outside and smoke a joint?" Santa asked.

"Sure," I said.

I usually didn't take people up on this kind of offer, especially in New York. A joint could be used as some sort of pick-up line and there was nothing more uncomfortable than a guy coming onto me after getting me stoned first. But this was Santa. The only threat he posed was a resemblance to all the childhood things I was learning to forget. I finished my drink, straight gin on ice, and followed Santa onto Amsterdam Avenue.

I hadn't really considered what it would be like to share a joint with Santa Claus on the corner of 90th and Amsterdam. I mean, down in the Village— no problem. Everybody dressed as Santa Claus was smoking off in a corner before hitting the streets again, ringing a bell, and asking people for change. But on the Upper West Side, people got kind of testy, especially when Santa Claus was on the corner getting stoned. And this was *Santa* getting stoned on the corner, not just some dude dressed up in a red suit on break from saying "ho ho ho" to the shopping mall kids on his lap. People might have thought he was a nut and belonged in the loony-bin, but he believed in himself and that was a hell of a lot more than I could say.

"I listened to Anselm Hollo read his poetry the other night," I said.

Santa was working on the joint.

"He said we are entering the dark ages again and it kind of made sense to me. I mean, maybe it's just the end of the century and all, but I can see how the immediate future holds a certain darkness. The way we communicate art is completely self-defeating and everyone thinks they've seen it all and we have seen it all and none of it is worthwhile. I think it's our point of view and our consciousness that needs changing."

Santa passed me the joint.

"I don't follow you, son."

"You know," I said in that hold-in-the-dope way, "you said you're fading because people don't believe in you anymore."

"Yes," he said. "Let me show you something."

I took another hit off the joint while Santa leaned over to unlace his boot. He struggled a bit with his big belly and cold fingers, blood rushing to his head, but he finally got the boot unlaced. I released the smoke slowly from my lungs as he pulled it off. His foot wasn't there. I could see the white fuzzy cuff at the bottom of the pant leg, and the pant leg hung like it was molding around a shin, but there was no ankle or foot. I could just see the sidewalk and his black boot.

I handed the joint back to Santa Claus.

"Go ahead," he said. "Touch it. It's there, but you just can't see it."

"No—no," I said. "I trust you. I see what you mean."

Santa shoved his invisible foot back into the boot. He took a deep drag off the joint. I looked at the half-moon poking out of the sky just above the building rooftops. Santa offered me another hit.

"No thanks," I said. "I've had enough."

"You see," he said. "I'm really fading. It started with my toenails and it's been slowly moving up my body. This year, it's to mid-thigh."

He put out the joint with his forefinger and dropped the roach in his front pocket as he looked up at the dim moon and sighed heavily.

"It gets worse when I don't drink," he said.

"Yeah," I replied, squinting at the moon as if that would help.

"I'm fading," Santa Claus said. "But the booze slows it down."

Santa laced up his boot and we went back into The Place. There were still a few hours till last call.

NAZIS AT THE CYNDI LAUPER CONCERT

jonathan montgomery

I went to the Cyndi Lauper concert alone because no one else was enthusiastic enough about 1980s pop music to pay forty dollars for a ticket. I don't like doing things by myself, but I had to go since her 1984 hit, "Time After Time," is my favorite song.

"Time After Time" is a song about someone loving you no matter what. Most people will love you for a time, but then that time runs out and it's the next time, and in that time they don't love you anymore. But "Time After Time" promises to love you the time after that time ad infinitum and I've always wanted that.

Two old people were in the seats next to me. A man and a woman with gray hair and wrinkles. They looked so old they had probably been old even in 1984. I found it hard to believe that we liked the same music.

I'd only seen Cyndi Lauper on TV before and wasn't sure if she was an actual person who could actually exist in front of you, but there she was on the stage. It was fascinating, and I should've wanted to watch her as much as possible, but I couldn't stop looking at the old man instead. He was bald and had a big fat nose and huge eyeglasses. He was wearing a thick sweater even though it was warm that night. I assumed he came from a world that was unlike mine in every way and he took Caribbean cruises and watched golf on television and drove an Oldsmobile and never analysed pop culture. Neither him nor the woman next to him smiled or seemed excited by the concert at all.

Cyndi took a break between songs to tell us how homosexual kids get kicked out of their homes by unsympathetic parents and have no place to go. And how she helped to create and fund a shelter that supports them. She told the audience we're all part of one human race and we should love each other even though we have differences. It made me feel good and I started thinking of ways I could be nicer to people.

But the old man was noticeably uncomfortable. He was shifting around in his chair and snorting. He whispered a comment to the old woman and then they both shook their heads.

Then he suddenly yelled out, "STOP TALKING AND PLAY SOME MUSIC!"

It was loud and people nearby turned back to look at him. Some of them even looked at me because they thought I'd said it.

It was supposed to be The Era of The New Awesome Accepting Culture, but the old man had just ruined everything. It made me want to shout at him, "What, you hate gays or something? Don't *you* want to be accepted? Don't you want someone to love *you* no matter what? It works both ways you know. And how the fuck don't you understand that the music and the talking have the same message? Is your mind so unsophisticated that it can only take in a catchy chord progression and nothing more? If you're that unsophisticated you should know it and feel self-conscious and not open up your stupid mouth at all. Why the fuck are you here? I want to wipe you from existence. I want to eliminate you and your kind from the world, you Nazi!"

Cyndi Lauper continued to talk about tolerance and the old man and woman rose from their seats. I wanted to tell them to sit back down and be better people. And when the old man gestured for me to stand up and let them pass through I pretended like I didn't notice and stayed seated. After a moment they realized I wasn't getting up and they had to go ahead anyway. The old man grunted in frustration as his awkward and stiff body had to shuffle through the tight gap between my knees and the seat in front of us. The woman also grunted and stumbled and had to reluctantly put a hand on my shoulder to stay balanced. As she took her final step past me her foot caught on my leg. It caused her to wobble helplessly for a moment before falling with a shriek to the floor.

She lay there moaning in shock in the aisle. I was glad she tripped and didn't assist her. The old man had to do it himself. He had to bend his rickety, painful, old back slowly down and grab and lift her. It took a while and he grumbled the whole time he did it. When she was finally up, they left and didn't return.

I felt proud of myself for not getting up for them. And for the rest of the concert I thought about how much I hated them.

Cyndi did not perform "Time After Time."

PASSING ON A TRADITION

manijeh badiozamani

The summer before my sophomore year in high school, my family rented a vacation place in the village of Maygoon, tucked in the mountains, roughly a two-hour drive east of Tehran. We were to share this place with the Davar family—Mrs. Davar was my father's second cousin. This summer place was on a fifteen-acre walled piece of property turned into an orchard. The house itself was only two very large, plain, empty rooms made of bricks and cement. A raised veranda extended in front of both rooms. There was no kitchen. The only outhouse, with a wooden door, was located in a corner on the west end of the property. A narrow stream ran through the orchard and our drinking water was hauled in every day from a nearby well. There was nothing else. Bare essentials for the duration of our stay were brought in from the city.

I don't know what prompted my parents to rent this place. Maybe they were plotting to test how their children fared in a camp-like condition for two months. It was a test of endurance and survival disguised as getting away from the scorching heat of summer in Tehran.

Maybe my father's intent was not only to get away from the heat, but also to teach us a lesson and make us appreciate the comfort of our home. But we were oblivious to all the shortcomings of the place and the subtle lessons we were supposed to learn.

Mr. Davar and my father hiked, played backgammon, and discussed the possibility of buying this piece of property. They spent hours inspecting the orchard and counting the trees. They were taking inventory just in case they decided to purchase the place.

Our main source of entertainment was the steady stream of visitors who showed up without prior notice. Relatives and friends who had been invited to drop in accepted the invitation without hesitation. They usually stayed for a night or two, escaping the heat of the city. They brought plenty of food, sleeping bags, and camped out on the property. They also brought their children, all younger than me.

One weekend, our neighbor in Tehran showed up with her two daughters. Sheila, the older one, was nearly twelve years old. She was an extremely attractive girl, a bit on the chubby side, with long black hair and gorgeous eyes and long dark lashes.

On that memorable afternoon, when all the grown-ups were taking naps after a heavy meal and the younger children were scattered around the orchard, I was stretched on a rug at the far end of the veranda reading a novel. Suddenly, several children came running and with a mixture of anxiety and excitement announced there was trouble at the outhouse. They reported Sheila had locked herself inside and was not coming out unless I went there and talked to her. Reluctantly, but with a tinge of curiosity, I put down my book and walked towards the outhouse, followed by six little boys and girls of various ages. Chattering constantly, they complained about not being able to use the outhouse because of Sheila.

I knocked on the wooden door and called her name. Upon hearing my voice, Sheila unlocked the door and let me in. Standing in a corner of that semi-lit place, she was trembling and looked pale as a ghost. I could see panic in her big brown eyes. She was holding her underpants in her hand. Without a word, she stretched her arms and showed me her underwear with blood stains.

I chuckle every time I think of what happened next. Just like my aunt, who had slapped me on the face several years earlier when I started my period, I smiled from ear to ear, and slapped Sheila on the face, on both cheeks! If I had not smiled, I'm sure the poor girl would have fainted thinking she was being punished for some unknown sin she had committed. However, with an aura of authority and confidence, still smiling, I explained to her, just the way it was explained to me, that the slapping of the face would bring her good luck and that it would also preserve her rosy cheeks. What on earth slapping had to do with menstruation and a rosy complexion, I didn't know. I was merely passing on a tradition.

I assured Sheila she was not sick and had done nothing wrong. By this time, the children were banging on the door, demanding an explanation. A few were threatening to pee in their pants. Quickly, we had to come up with a story. I opened the door and calmly announced there was a bullfrog in the outhouse and it had frightened Sheila. It was the only excuse I could think of at that particular moment. Immediately, I regretted my choice when all the children screamed with excitement and rushed in to see the bullfrog.

METALLIC BOND

sharon frantz

I look up at the creak of my door and find Nessa standing there, holding up the big black makeup bag. I nod, granting her access. I shut my door so the rest of the dorm won't see what we're doing.

"Doesn't this feel weird to you?" I ask.

Nessa sighs and spills the bag's contents on my bed. "Of course it feels weird. But what was I supposed to do? Say no thanks?"

"What exactly did she say?"

"Nothing, really," Nessa says, "just shoved the bag in my face and asked if I would use it. Didn't even wait for an answer."

I allow myself to glance over the scattered makeup and nail polish. A tube of eyeliner catches my eye and I move to grab it—eyeliner is a small weakness of mine—but pull back. Nessa watches, silent. She had to carry the bag—there was no way she was going to make the first move.

"That looks like a good color for you," she says.

I shoot what I hope is a nasty look and reconsider the eyeliner. The color label is facing me.

"Smokey topaz," I say. More interesting than black. Black eyeliner is so obvious. I shake away the thoughts and stare down Nessa.

"Oh fine," she says and glances over the pile. She picks up gold nail polish. "Do you want this?"

I shake my head. "I have some."

She sets it aside and dives back into the pile for my smokey topaz eyeliner. Throwing it beside me, she says, "You can have dibs on the eyeliner."

"Shouldn't she be keeping this? Mary has to mind."

"When have you ever seen her wear makeup?" Nessa asks, waving blush in my face. I shake my head again and she puts it in her pile. As she starts flipping through a stack of eye shadow, I spot a metallic tube. I hesitate, then pick it up and I wonder what I could possibly do with silver eyeliner.

"She's acting like it's a job, getting rid of it all," I say, putting the eyeliner in my pile.

"It *is* her job. Her dad asked her to."

"Yeah, but it's like... it's like she's not even thinking about it. Just throwing stuff at us and trying to act like she's cleaning out the attic, like nothing happened."

Nessa shrugs, setting a bottle of peacock-blue nail polish on her growing pile. "She knows my door is open if she wants to talk."

"But she doesn't ask for anything."

I have no idea what the look she gives me means. She starts opening a few more compacts, testing colors. Nessa throws one at me and I examine it—an unnamed trio of grays. I hear a creak, but it doesn't register until I realize there is a body standing beside me.

"That would work well for that smokey-eye thing

you like," Mary says.

Nessa shifts and drops an arm, trying to hide her pile from view. I don't have much of a pile to hide, but seeing as I'm the one currently holding the contraband, it doesn't really matter.

"Nessa just gave it to me," I say, dropping it near, but not in, my pile. Nessa sighs and I twist the corner of my comforter around my hand, waiting for something.

We all scan the makeup. Nessa's arm twitches, but she doesn't reach for anything. I find a tube of concealer that is too dark to ever match my skin tone, but I keep staring at it. I imagine Mary wondering how we could be picking through the makeup like we were and taking things that don't belong to us and not thinking at all about where they came from, and then Mary points and says, "You should try that one."

I refocus on a shimmery liquid lilac. I pick it up and claim it, pushing the gray trio into my pile at the same time.

Nessa resumes sorting and this time I join her, looking through some tubes of lipstick and gloss I'd been curious about.

Contemplating the color of the last one, dusty rose, I look at Mary and start to imagine a woman I've never met, replacing Mary's liquid brown, natural eyes with heavily-lined dull ones looking out from under shimmering lids. I put her in glasses so the reflecting light will show my grimy dorm wall rather than bloodshot eyes that won't be fixed with anything from the pile. Hid, maybe, but not fixed. Her complexion is bright and free but darker than mine—dark enough for that concealer that nobody will use. Too dark for the color in my hand, but it will work just the same.

"This would be a great color for you," I say, offering the tube.

She takes it, her hand lingering in mine for just a moment.

THE COMEDY ACT

corin balkovek

What's a dentist's favorite instrument?

A tuba toothpaste.

Why do shoemakers go to heaven?

They all have good soles.

Why does a chicken coop have only two doors?

Because if it had four, they would call it a chicken sedan.

My father knew them all. If it was based on pun, he loved it. A clever turn-of-phrase, even better. Inside his head he had amassed a collection of terrible jokes the size of which would make a Catskills comedian go green.

What did the sink say to the leaky faucet?

You're a real drip.

I didn't get to see him much, my father. My parents split back in the dark days before I started remembering things. She moved to Oregon, remarried, and started a new family around me, giving me a host of half siblings I never really wanted. He moved to Arizona, stayed single and opened up his own barber shop. Every summer, he would shut down the shop for three days, hop in his grumbling Chevy truck and drive the 1,300 miles to pick me up for my annual two month visit. After a few hours sleeping in a hotel, he'd then turn around and drive 1,300 miles back, only this time with a captive audience.

How do you make a witch itch?

Take away her W.

As a child, I loved the jokes. They would send me into hysterics, doubled over until my head hit the cracked vinyl of the truck's bench seat next to my knees. My favorites were the ones he told over and over—his favorites too, I guess—because then I could chime in with the punchline.

What time is it when an elephant sits on your fence?

Time to get a new fence.

Once I got to be a teenager, I hated the jokes, almost as much as I hated going to Arizona. While my friends got to spend the summer at the lake or sleeping the day away, I had to spend it alone with my father and a host of road-crossing chickens and idiots who didn't know how to screw in a light bulb.

There was one joke in particular that he liked to save up during the drive. About a third of the way through the journey, as we cut through the center of California, the highway rolling past epic orchards and fields, we would pass a billboard the shape of a gigantic pumpkin. "Morton's Pumpkin Patch and Corn Maze—Open September til' December." The moment he spotted the big orange bulb sprouting in the horizon, my father would crack:

How do you fix a broken jack-o-lantern?

With a pumpkin patch.

The summer of my fifteenth year, without fail, he told that joke. And rather than join in on the punchline or force myself to chuckle, I exploded with all the indignant rage a hormone-riddled teenager can produce: "Jesus, could you please stop telling that stupid joke! Or how about all the jokes! God, why can't you just buy a radio for this piece of crap and join the rest of the world in the 20th century?" I spent the rest of the trip and the summer locked away in my adolescent discontent. After that, my father would just buy me a bus ticket to Arizona. A few years later, my mother and I flew to Arizona to collect his ashes and bring him to the home in Oregon he never lived in.

It's late November and I'm quietly whisking down the freeway, driving through the sheets of rainwater being thrown up over my car by passing semis. After hours of fussing and crying, my daughter sits back quietly in her car seat and I'm afraid turning on the radio will rile her up again, so I drive in silence, thinking. I calculate how much longer the drive will be to my sister's house, I wonder how she's going to manage to squeeze our now over-sized family into her home for Thanksgiving dinner. I think about how much this road has changed since my youth, those orchards of citrus fruit and almonds bearing instead miles of strip malls and fast food restaurants, each in a row, each identical to one another.

And then, I spot it. It's no longer in the shape of a pumpkin, but instead a standard rectangle sign with over-sized pictures of adorable children and families smiling and holding up their orange loot. "Morton's Pumpkin Patch and Laser Tag—Open Year Round!"

"Hey, Mirabelle." In the rear-view mirror, I can see my daughter's curly head perk up, pulled out of her lolling daydreaming.

"How do you fix a broken jack-o-lantern?"

"How, Mommy?" she asks after a period of silence. The answer catches in my throat. It pushes up through my eyes and slides silently down my cheeks.

WELCOME TO THE FANTASY HAND JOB BROTHEL

nancy stohlman

Have you ever wanted to get a hand job from Abraham Lincoln? How about Gandhi, Bette Midler or Don Knotts? Here at the Fantasy Hand Job Brothel, we specialize in making all your fantasy hand jobs come true.

We use the term "hand job" interchangeably with both our male and female clients, and sexual orientation doesn't bother us. Why hand jobs? Because a hand job is simple and doesn't violate any of the new prostitution codes or spread STDs, and hey, who doesn't want to say they've gotten a hand job from Helen Keller? Keeping everything legal and safe allows you to stop worrying about getting busted and start concentrating on the real task in front of you—getting off.

I started Fantasy Hand Job Brothel 15 years ago when I realized that most "fantasies" were limited to 20-year olds in silky lingerie or sweaty, bare-chested fireman. But what if you secretly desire a hand job from Barry Manilow? What are you to do about it? Hide it away in a shameful place, jerk off to busty blonde twins just like the rest of the world? Just think: an individual as varied and unique as yourself, jerking off to the exact same thing as everyone else on the planet? *Now* how unique do you feel?

Don't get me wrong: A classic hand job is a lovely thing, and we have Playboy bunnies and Chippendales and Dallas Cowboy cheerleaders to name a few. We also cater to traditionalists, and so we have Marilyn Monroe, James Dean, Elvis Presley and Mae West, as well as our new two-for-one Brangelina hand job.

But maybe you, like millions of others, secretly want a hand job from Genghis Khan. Or maybe it's Martha Stewart (who also comes as jailbird Martha). The point is, when you want a hand job from Rick Moranis or Oprah Winfrey, we've got it.

Like politics? How about a hand job from FDR or Eleanor Roosevelt? If history is more your thing, try Henry VIII, Marie Curie or Marquis de Sade. Like radical politics? How about a hand job from Angela Davis, Ché Guevara, Karl Marx or Malcolm X?

And if you're into philanthropy, what about Mother Teresa?

Still suffering from your childhood religious scarring? We have both skinny and fat Buddha, Mary Magdalene, Joseph Smith and several Hindu gods, including Vishnu and Lakshmi. (Any other god can be designed for you with 48 hours notice.) And if you're on your period, we have a special "Moses Parts the Red Sea" fantasy hand job.

Need a gift for your college graduate? How about a hand job from Albert Einstein? Something special for your mother's 60th birthday? Why not get her that hand job from Tom Selleck or Tom Jones that she's always wanted? A unique wedding gift? What about his and hers hand jobs from Romeo and Juliet?

Country western fans will be pleased to get our Dolly Parton/Kenny Rogers combo, and the English professor in your life will love our line of literary figures, from Captain Ahab to Alice in Wonderland!

From Dionne Warwick to Charlie Chaplin, the fun never ends at the Fantasy Hand Job Brothel.

Like something just freaky? How about a hand job from Picasso or Michael Jackson?

Whatever you can fantasize, we can make it come true.

Upcoming specials:

Gifts of the Magi: Get a hand job complete with gold, frankincense and myrrh from our own three kings, and during the month of December buy two kings and get the third free.

Luck of the Irish: Want a hand job from a leprechaun? He'll have you kissing the blarney stone and then some.

Kitchen Gourmet: Julia Childs will not only give you a great, homemade hand job, but she'll whip up a batch of brownies—with or without nuts.

Beethoven's Birthday Month: Visit Beethoven in December and sing your very own "Ode to Joy!"

On Golden Pond: Celebrate your Golden Anniversary with "Golden" showers on Katharine Hepburn or Henry Fonda… or both!

New for 2011: Satan!

We at Fantasy Hand Job Brothel think everyone is entitled to a good hand job now and then. So from George Burns to George Clinton, from Harriet Tubman to Queen Elizabeth, come on down to the Fantasy Hand Job Brothel today and leave satisfied.

- » All Fantasy hand job participants must be at least 18 years old.
- » Please give 48 hours notice on all specialty hand jobs.
- » You may schedule no more than four hand jobs per day for insurance reasons.
- » All hand jobs are limited to 30 minutes and "results" are not guaranteed.

THE GHOST GETS A VISIT

robert scotellaro

"I was The Ghost," he said to the woman sitting next to him on the edge of the bed. There was a small TV playing on a chair across from them. A soap opera. A young actress weeping and some guy in a suit sweet-talking her into or out of something—she couldn't tell which.

"That was my moniker," he said, pointing to a shrine-like clutter of framed photos of him thirty years younger. One, with another wrestler he held over his head as easily as a bag of laundry.

"Wow," she said. "Great outfit."

"It was mostly a sheet. A fancy one with cut-outs. A rhinestone collar. Silk, though. The sheet was real silk. I was always slipping out of holds. Disappearing sort of. That's why they called me The Ghost."

"Quite a Hall of Fame," she said.

"I was something once," he said.

Jerry the desk clerk had told her he wouldn't quibble over the price. The Ghost could play it any way he wanted, she thought. Hey, yapping counted, if that's all it was.

She saw him glance down briefly at her breasts. "They're all mine," she said.

He patted his chest. "That makes two of us," he said, referring to the colossal avalanche that had occurred.

"Gravity's a bitch," she said, tapping her rear.

He smiled. There were a couple of teeth missing. "Wasn't always like that," he said. "Was a time I could rip a phone book in half, easy as shit."

"You mind if I light up?"

He shrugged.

She took a long puff and blew the smoke out of the corner of her mouth, away from him.

"You read that one yet?" She reached down picking a slim paperback from a stack of them by the side of the bed.

"Read 'em all," he said.

"Think you can rip this one in half?"

"You kidding? Here, give me that other one, too." He lined up the two slender novels and worked his enormous hands around them, twisting back and forth. He bit his lip till a small tear in the pages widened. After a great effort, the books split apart.

"Wow!" she said, one eye squinted shut from the cigarette in her mouth, and clapped. She squeezed his bicep with what little of her hand she could wrap around it. "You still got it," she said.

"Small potatoes," he said, tossing the book pieces down. "I bet I could lift you over my head and hold you there with one hand."

She gazed at him for a moment without speaking.

"I'll hold you over the bed if you like."

She took a long drag, then let her cigarette drop into an empty beer can on the floor. "Okay, I guess.

But you be careful. You be damn careful," she cautioned.

"No sweat," he said, having her lie flat on the bed with her arms at her sides. "Make your body stiff," he said. "Yeah, like that."

He put his hands under her, drew in a few deep breaths. She closed her eyes and felt the world drop away, and when she opened them again she was staring at the ceiling. She heard him grunt as he gingerly took one hand away. She turned her head and could see the veins in his neck bulged out—his face red and contorted.

"Don't move," he said, his voice tight. Almost imperceptibly, he turned her shakily to the left and then the right.

"*Oh, Daddy*," she said. "*Oh, Daddy*." And she thought she heard him groan, but it was muffled and indistinct. She tilted, bracing herself as his arm dipped. But he grabbed her quickly with both hands again and lowered her down slowly into the sheets.

She lay there quietly and watched him huffing and swaying like a giant that had just jumped off a carousel. Noticed a tattoo dagger twitch as he stood there. Then he sat in a chair by the wall and slowly took off his shoes. Then his pants. Got up and draped them over the TV.

The actress in the soap was in a different scene by a marina. Tearless now, she was letting somebody really have it. But the woman watching, as The Ghost approached, could no longer tell who.

SERRATED

e. b. giles

The leaves are a crisp brutal green, jagged as a serrated blade. But it's the berries that draw me in: those plump, bright, bursting berries so red I ache to place them on my tongue. What will that red taste like? I must know. These were the berries Mother told me were okay to eat, weren't they? They look the same, but maybe the leaves on that bush were not quite as thick... or waxy... or sharp... But the small round berries look the same.

I pluck one from the bush. The break is not clean, and the berry oozes thick where it comes away from the stem. I place it delicately on my tongue and let it sit there a moment. I press the berry to the roof of my mouth bursting it. The flavor is sweet, with a trace of bitterness, and the liquid prickles my tongue. The red is so entrancing I can't stop. I pluck another, then another, chasing berries and hording them up in my greedy fists. Then I pack my mouth and crunch the exploding berries into a mass of bitter-laced sweetness. As I chew, my tongue goes from tingling to dead-numb until I can chew no longer. The roof of my mouth, my gums, even my teeth vanish into nothingness. The blue ice of panic floods my veins. I slap hands to my face to see if my cheeks and jaw still exist. I try to spit, but the red mashed mess dribbles from my mouth leaving a crimson trail down the white front of my down coat. I stick fingers in my mouth to pull out the last of the swollen mass, and I scrape cheeks that I cannot feel. Am I pulling out berries or skin and blood?

I stand still and stare at the sky. I try to forget my bleeding cheeks. Clouds fight across pale blue, waging a battle complete with swords clashing shields and the deafening cries of war. I frown hard and clear the clouds away with my mind until the sky is uninterrupted blue. The sun materializes when the clouds have vanished. It races toward me, and then it is right up close to my face, warming my skin, and melting away the numb feeling in my face.

"What do you want, little one?" he asks. "To dance with me?"

Dancing. Was that my idea or Sun's? I can't remember, but it's a good idea so I nod. "Let's dance then," Sun says, taking my hands in his fiery tendrils.

Music lifts from underground and fills me with a throbbing tempo. We spin, Sun and I, and the movement elates me.

I hear words: "I want to dance! I want to dance!" A dark, spiky tree uproots itself. Tree cuts in, and his branches don't feel nearly as nice in my hands as Sun's, but I want to be a good sport so I hold the branches even though they cut my palms and cause beads of blood to spring up in my deathly white hands. A masked raccoon scurries into sight, stands on his hind legs, and sniffs the air. We stop dancing.

"Hello, Raccoon."

"Hello, Your Highness," he says, with a bow.

I am the princess in this enchanted land, and Sun and Tree and Raccoon are my royal subjects. Did I already know that? Raccoon's dark fur blossoms with white cotton. All I want in the world is to touch that fur.

"What can I do for you?" he asks.

That fur! It is so soft it hurts my eyes. I ache to touch it. I reach out my hand, but I'm spinning dizzy. I ache, like I've never ached for anything in my life— save the berries. Those too-bright red berries sprayed across the too-bright green leaves. Those serrated knife edge leaves.

I pluck berries. Stuff them in my mouth. Feel them bursting and sweet and bitter and flesh-numbing. The dizziness presses in on me. My head is pounding. The trees and the sun and blue sky whirl around me. The snowy ground reaches up to slap me across the face. My stare is vacant. My deathly white hands are twisted beneath me. A puddle of too-bright red stains crisp white snow.

SHEDDING

kenneth pobo

Jerry slams the door that leads to the porch.

"Damn that Jeff! When he wants to know something, it's like he puts me on a witness stand. Yes, Your Honor, I forgot to get milk. No, Your Honor, I didn't take the coats to the cleaners."

The birds aren't listening, though they seem happy enough, a hummingbird sipping red liquid, three wrens near the wisteria.

When he's frustrated, Jerry cleans. Today it's the shed. The attic is stuffed as Jeff is a pack rat and "can't bear" to throw things away. "We might need it someday," he says. Jerry doesn't know when a broken trellis will be needed, but it's up there behind Christmas ornaments.

The shed is one of those pre-built structures. You point where it should go. The guys unload it. You have iced tea and they leave. The main item it houses is the lawn tractor. Jerry and Jeff hate mowing, so they pay Jeff's nephew Barton to do it. Barton, 14, hates gays but loves money.

When they got the house, Jerry had a suitcase

filled with pictures and mementos from his pre-Jeff life. Love letters. Pictures of him and Steve in Key West, bearded heads photographed on the wooden bodies of bikini women. It seemed hysterical at the time.

He kept the suitcase.

He put it in the shed, in the back. Jeff rarely goes out there, so it seemed like a good place to store it.

In his fury at Your Honor, he rearranges a stand holding shovels and hoes. He picks up dried leaves from the previous autumn. With no bag, he sprinkles them on the lawn. Barton or the wind will make short work of them.

He sees the suitcase.

He remembers boyfriends before Steve, a 10-weeker named Darryl, who was quite good in bed. But quite boring at the kitchen table. Wasn't there a card Darryl had sent him that said, "For a bottom, you're the tops!" Why would he have saved that?

Why even think about it now?

Jerry navigates carefully behind the lawn tractor, big and bulky, green like a smashed grasshopper. The suitcase, dusty and moldy, makes Jerry queasy, but he's made it this far.

When he opens it, mice skitter out. It has become a nest. He shivers as he drops the case and escapes from the shed, banging his knee against the lawn tractor.

After catching his breath, he notices on the side of the shed the first heavenly blue morning glories just opening. Only three blooms, but a whole bunch of buds waiting to turn late August into a petal lake. Heavenly indeed.

"Jerry, the phone! It's your mom."

"Be right there."

Jerry quickly returns to the shed and retrieves the case, holding it far from his body as he fears an errant mouse may scurry out. He drops it in the black trash can on his way back in the house.

"Hi, Mom. No, nothing new here."

Jeff is making scrambled eggs and bacon and humming. He holds a knife as if it's a mic and starts crooning "Things I'd Like To Say," a 1968 hit, a ballad.

"Baby, baby, there's things I'd like to say…"

Jerry thinks there are things he'd like to say too, but he's talking to Mom now and that may go on a while. Things that wouldn't be said to Your Honor, but to Jeff. About morning glories. Or nothing at all, nothing more than a weather update.

When he hangs up, the eggs are ready. They sit at their usual places and dig in.

"I found an old suitcase in the shed. Mice were in it!"

Burying his head in the Sports section, Jeff says, "Eeew." He enjoys few things more than the Sunday paper. Jerry looks out the window and sees that the birds are still busy feeding. The eggs are particularly good. He feels lighter, even in a house with too much clutter on a hot August morning. A bit of blue appears right at the edge of the window.

A PLACE TO SLEEP

nick kimbro

It's been a long time since they slept in each other's arms, but he wakes with her clawing against his chest. It's the middle of the night; their first in the new bed. "What's wrong?" he asks. She murmurs something and he rubs the back of her neck, saying *Shhhh* until she is awake enough to speak.

The dream was of him dying—not once, but twice. She can't remember how it happened the first time, only waking in a sweat and pacing at the foot of the bed, questioning whether or not she should wake him. She stands beside the bed and shakes him by the shoulder, although he doesn't respond. She shakes him with two hands, but still he doesn't answer. She feels alone in the room. She tries to scream but all that comes out is a weak stream of air. She climbs back into bed screaming silently, unable to control her limbs. She lays her head on her pillow. Her legs grow numb, next her arms. She knows she is dying, and then she wakes.

"I thought that people weren't supposed to die in their dreams," he says, lying beside her in the dark.

He listens with his eyes closed. The way she describes it, he feels almost as if the dream were his.

"Maybe I didn't," she suggests. "Maybe I woke up just before."

They go back to sleep and when they wake the next morning he is squeezing her. She asks what's the matter. He says he can't remember.

She has an interview today, and he sits drinking coffee all morning on their balcony, waiting for her to return. The set of patio chairs is all they own besides the bed, and now they cannot sleep. She returns at noon and says they've invited her to a second interview on Monday. They have the weekend to themselves.

At night they lie awake. Most recently, he's died and gone to hell. She cut her wrists to follow, but landed in heaven instead.

"You're not allowed to do that," he insists. Something is wrong with her dreams. He gets up to fetch her a glass of water from the kitchen. She takes a sip and, to get her mind off of her own dream, asks what he was dreaming about. Again he doesn't remember.

Saturday and Sunday pass with him in the apartment. She wants to go to the farmer's market. She wants to try the church. He does not want to go to either of these places and does not want her to go either. He stays home and draws the blinds, wishes the walls were thicker, that there were more padlocks on the door. He does not want Monday to come, but Monday does come, and she silences her alarm clock without waking him. She has slept through the night. This is a good sign. She kisses him on the forehead before dressing.

At noon she returns with a bottle of André and

a smile, searching for him on the balcony although he isn't there. She pours them both mimosas, and takes them into the bedroom where he is as she left him. She sits his drink on the nightstand and tries to wake him. He does not respond. She sets her own drink down, and shakes him with both hands, but he just frowns into his pillow. She begins to panic and remembers the dream from several nights ago. She wonders if she is dreaming now. She lies down behind him and wraps her arms around his torso, shuts her eyes and recites a prayer to herself, trying to remember what she dreamed of last night. She cannot. Last night she slept as soundly as a stone, and no matter how hard she tries now, sleep will not find her.

AUNT STOKESIA'S 78TH BIRTHDAY

kenneth pobo

I never liked her. She's sententious. Oh, how I love that word. My high school senior English teacher, Mr. Pamwell, wrote it on my essay about T.S. Eliot. I said that Prufrock was clearly gay and couldn't wake up, preferred life as a dream. "Jerry, you are sententious. Do this over."

I didn't do it over. I took the D and ran. I looked up sententious. Immediately Aunt Stokesia's face flashed before me.

When she divorced Uncle Bill, who everyone in the family called Sweet William, which made him blush, she said she had no use for people who didn't read. He died too young, only 52. Aunt Stokesia, when told, shrugged. And drank more green tea. To no one's surprise, she never remarried.

She did have one thing that I adored—a milk-glass cigarette holder shaped like a top hat that held a dozen Tareyton cigarettes. I snuck those cigarettes when I got to be fourteen. She caught me and gave me hell.

I don't like being given hell. Or being given heaven. I like smoking. Or I did. I gave it up because my boyfriend Lenny said it was them or me. I chose badly, should've kept smoking. But, I lost both Lenny and a craving for nicotine.

Aunt Stokesia insists on white cake. She will not eat chocolate cake and claims it rots your stomach. Republicans are good. Democrats bad. Gardens good. TV bad. And the computer, HAW, she says, fuggetaboutit.

I have a terrible desire to throw my white cake right at her face. But I was raised to respect my elders. Why respect a sententious elder? Why not fart and leave? I stay. I eat all of it, ask for seconds. I actually like the cake.

Once I asked my mom if Aunt S was always this way. "Yeah, a complete bitch. I mean, not a nice lady. She thinks she's a queen."

Funny, I know I shouldn't say that I agree with her, that I'll catch hell if I say "You got that right." Mom isn't sententious, but she thinks there are two languages—one for grown-ups and one for kids, meaning people under twenty-one. I'm twenty.

These family parties would be funny if a doctor came in with syringes, gave us all truth serum, turned on a tape recorder, and asked us how we felt about Aunt Stokesia.

It might not be funny. She wouldn't care, I don't think. But what if she did? What if she hung her head and started crying and got up from the table, not even putting on her coat, and walking out into the chilly night—and us calling after her, "Please, Aunt Stokesia, please come back," but she vanishes into the darkness.

I will be 78 someday. Maybe. I could kick off

tomorrow, but I see myself at a table like this. Mom says that I don't realize how quickly it all goes. By "it" I guess she means life. Or looks. Or happiness.

Aunt Stokesia was twenty once. Was she dour, afraid to laugh, sentention? If so, who did this to her?

I have a strange desire to tell her I love her. It will pass. She'll open her mouth again, having carefully restored her lipstick from cake-smear, and say, "I mean, who or what is a Lady Gaga? After Sinatra, there's not been one good singer, not one."

And I will be thinking shut up, shut up, you drab barn door of a person. And wondering would she at least be polite if I brought a boyfriend to her next birthday party? Would any of them? Or would they smile like Mr. Pamwell handing me back my essay, like they had won something.

MY SISTER IS A LIVING STATUE IN THE FRENCH QUARTER

shellie zacharia

She plays classical violin on the street corner, but only one piece, and then she freezes. She stands with the violin tucked under her chin. People throw dollars and spare change into a gold instrument case. She doesn't say thank you, she doesn't smile, and she doesn't frown at the pennies that are like insults. She is spray-painted metallic gold. Everywhere: face, eyelids, hair, dress, shoes.

Someone says, "Play Cajun fiddle. This is Louisiana." The gold woman doesn't respond.

She can play a mean fiddle if she wants. My sister surprises me with her stillness. I have not seen her in a long time.

She was always in a crisis with some reason she needed money from our parents—loans for school, more school, a trip to Thailand, rehab, therapy, three weeks at an artists' colony.

"Why do you keep giving her money?" I once asked my mother.

"How can you not help someone you love," my mother said. She sighed and wrote checks, transferred funds, and my father, always a quiet man, just shook his head and said, "What else can we do?"

"Does she ever pay you back?" I asked.

"Yes," my mother paused, "a little at a time."

I asked for money one time. I hated asking. It took me days to finally make the call. I needed a loan for a business venture. I was tired of my job at the bookstore.

"Money is tight right now," my mother said. "Your sister and the recent surgery. She has no insurance, that little gallery she works for, you know. Maybe in a while."

I thought about my sister's partial hysterectomy, her call to me about how she felt cheated. "No babies," she said. "My life stinks."

"You're not married. You don't have any money," I said. "Maybe you don't need a baby."

"Fuck you."

"Fuck you too," I said and hung up.

"She's very talented," a man says. He is sunburned to a crawfish boil.

His knock-kneed wife says, "She's a street performer," and the way she says it, not with awe but with ugliness, I think my sister will break her statue stillness and rake fingers across the wife's fat face.

The last I heard my sister was living in Memphis. She could still be angry. Or ashamed. Maybe I am.

She may not recognize me. I've cut my hair short; I'm six months pregnant. My sunglasses cover most of my face, and I'm a few states from home.

"You know you can adopt," I had called to say after the last angry phone conversation. It was my form of apology.

"You're so damn nice," she said. She was drunk. I could tell by the way she slurred. "You and your perfectly mediocre world," she said when I didn't respond. "You need a real life."

"You too," I said and hung up. I waited for her to call back and apologize. She never did.

And now, more than two years later, a chance encounter. I'm wandering New Orleans while my husband is in a business conference; my sister is playing violin in the French Quarter. All that paint. Talent. My golden sister stares past me, above me, like I am just another face in the small crowd.

I could do the unexpected thing. I could push her off her gold crate. I could hug her.

I slide my sunglasses on top of my head. She moves. I swear she sees me. She begins to play. Her wrists are fragile. Bony. Too thin. I pull a $20 bill from my wallet and lay it in her gold case. "Brahms," I say, and I am gone.

DRIVING IN ROSEBUD

teresa milbrodt

The Sanskrit word for war translates into "the
desire for more cows," and as we drive through the
hills of South Dakota on the way home from your
job at the college you say that doesn't surprise you
because it's all about cows—cash cows and sacred
cows and waiting until the cows come home—but
you get quiet and I know you're thinking about wars,
little wars with bottles and big wars with governments
and none of them end, including your personal war
about what to do tomorrow when the lady who lives
a mile down the road will come to the door with
a block of commodity cheese and her grandfather's
old beaded coup stick and want fifty bucks for both
of them, and you'll give her sixty because you're that
kind of nice, and you'll hang the coup stick on the wall
because the fight happens in other ways now, through
e-mails and federal legislation but the struggle is the
same, life and death and heart disease and diabetes
and long waits in the IHS hospital that I only hear
about at work, but your best friend's husband was
sent away from the doctor to another clinic when he

had the heart attack in the car while driving with his daughter, but he managed to pull over and save her on the shoulder while he passed away, and this is the new genocide, easier to overlook since it comes in ones and twos and yearly statistics, because the war continues in a desire for more cows and trees and mountains and pages of names to forget, but I know everyone remembers them here, repeats them in their sleep and at the office and at the bar and in the casino bingo hall where they sit in Pall Mall smoke with Daubers and Diet Cokes and twenty-five dollars worth of hope for new miracles. I don't know how you stand it, a New Orleans transplant who saw twenty-two Mardi Gras and lived to tell about it, who swore she'd never live outside the Big Easy until coming here, a two day's drive north, and you discovered it was home because your car would not let you leave, wound up with another mechanic every time you headed south, so you resigned yourself to harsh summers and harsher winters and the handful of silver days in between, because even when the guys at work kill two rattlesnakes in the field beside the campus technology building, when you come home you can watch the sunset from your trailer window and the horses in silhouette, because you won this isolated beauty that sometimes prevents you from leaving the house for four days in January, it's what everyone won, a door prize in the middle of nowhere with trailers like Easter eggs hidden in the hills and pow-wows at the end of five miles of gravel road with beef vegetable soup and fry bread and yellow cake with chocolate icing, because you have to focus on what was retained, maintained, sustained, how, despite Custer's best efforts, people are still here, still breathing, so even we as outsiders count those small victories in the forgotten and ongoing war, and we know we are not saviors but we are here to listen, to do what we can, even if that means making beignets every year at the Sundance and working on grant applications to build more log homes, there are many small ways of fighting when so much of the war is to make it to tomorrow.

LIFE WITH ROSES

janice peebly

1970—I am the last of my three roommates to leave the apartment in El Paso. It means I have to do the terminal cleaning, but I don't mind because John and I get to have a quiet dinner for our last night. In the morning, he leaves for Germany and I am off to Hawaii. I take a picture of a single red rose in a green glass Coke bottle on the kitchen table of the clean apartment on my way out the door.

1971—Finally, after three days and two nights I can sleep on my stomach for the first time in nine months. The first thing I see when I wake up is a dainty arrangement of blue and white carnations in a baby blue ceramic shoe; one petite white rose peeks out from the middle of the arrangement. I tell my mother how pretty they are when I call that afternoon. "Why didn't you call earlier?" she asks, "I've been frantic all day." I was alone and five thousand miles from home.

1978—Flowers come for me while I am at work. They look odd there on our dining room table, among the school books, hats and scarves, Josh's match box cars. "But, why don't you want to go out with him?" my mother asks. She looks pointedly at the flowers, a vulnerable mix of red and white carnations with one single red rose in the center. I whine. "He holds me too tight when we dance." I can feel a persistent bulge against my middle. I don't tell my mother that; I can't tell her that.

1989—The box from Breitingers flower shop waits on the dining room table. It is a lovely spring day in May. Josh is in the bathroom shaving for the second time that day. His rented tux hangs on the bathroom door hook. I ease off the cream colored satin ribbon and lift the lid. The heady aroma of gardenia fills the room. I inhale deeply, thinking that one breath of that amazingly sweet flower will have to last me for the rest of my life.

1990—I stopped hating funeral homes sometime around 1986. Memories of satiny white roses cascading over the side of dark mahogany wood, and then the next year giant fuzzy white chrysanthemums blend together with these delicate daisies and baby's breath that dwarf a tiny wooden box.

1994—A dozen yellow roses were delivered today. Somewhere, sometime, I said I loved yellow roses. I don't know why I said it. I don't particularly love yellow ones, any more than pink ones or white ones. I don't like red ones much anymore. Their deep red essence, so like blood, disturbs me. They ask too much, but these yellow roses look lonely against the bare table top. I lay my head down on my arms and cry.

2010—Today, I bought a dozen white roses at King Soopers. Their tight creamy buds held so much promise, I couldn't resist. I put them in a tall red vase, place them on the dining room table and sit down to watch them. They open quickly in the warmth of the room and as they open some of them have a faint pink blush in the center. A reflection of the red vase, maybe. For some reason, as I sit there watching the rose petals relax, I remember that single red rose in a green Coke bottle forty years ago and I wonder what happened to the time.

CIRCULATION DESK

thomas mundt

Today I'm covering Phyllis' morning shift at the Circulation Desk because her husband fell down a flight of stairs last night and she's still at Silver Cross Hospital, probably spoon-feeding him or reading him the *Joliet Herald* sports section. This means I have to open the library, make sure the Checkout Terminals are functioning properly and the Oprah Book Club Section near the entrance is in order.

It sounds like more work than it is. It takes me less than a second to power-up the Terminals because all it takes is the flip of a switch. And, it takes me exactly zero seconds to get the Oprah Book Club Section in order because there are never any Oprah Book Club Books to dust or rearrange. They're always checked out or waitlisted because they're the only books any of the adults in our town read. That, and anything that ends with ...*for Dummies*.

I finish my less-than-a-second of work early, just to get it out of the way. Then I take my post at my terminal and take out my pocket-size *101 Easy Crossword Puzzles* book. I'm about to get started when

Randy the maintenance guy sidles up. It's Saturday, so he's not in his uniform. He's wearing jeans and one of those Big Johnson t-shirts, the ones that say things like *Big Johnson Surfboards: It's Not How You Ride the Waves… It's the Size of Your Johnson That Counts!* Randy's shirt says *Big Johnson Fishing* but there are a bunch of nacho stains and tears on the catch phrase.

I can tell Randy wants to use my terminal for something.

"Mind if I…"

Randy "asks," but he's not really asking. He pulls my terminal's keyboard in front of him, starts typing away.

"Ummm…"

Randy shoots me a look. I can tell that whatever it is he's doing, he's not supposed to be doing it. I look down at my keyboard and notice that Randy's fingertips are leaving black smudges all over it.

Randy keeps typing and typing until he hits Enter three times in a row, laughs.

"She's all yours, Ass Crammer."

Randy slides the keyboard back into place hard, like he's mad at it. He's still laughing as he walks toward the boiler room. Then he starts whistling and I think it might be Foghat but I can't tell for sure.

When I look at my terminal's screen, I see that Randy ran an Author Query with "Nicholas Sparks" as his Search Term. There's a full page of results but I notice a "check" next to *The Notebook*, which means the book's description has been changed. I double-click on *"The Notebook"* and a new description window pops up. It reads, "pussy ass bitch shit u read b/c u r a fagot or b/c u r old."

I consider deleting it but I don't. Instead, I picture the pain-in-the-ass old lady who's always wearing the puffy-paint *Born to Raise Collies* sweatshirt, the one that said all those bad things about Asians that one time, reading it on a U-Check-It and stroking out. I see her calling the Mokena Public Library Patron Information Line the second she comes to, hear her leave an angry voicemail about how the library's staffed with degenerates, how America's no better than one of the -stan countries these days.

I put the crossword puzzles on hold and search for more Randy descriptions. I type "Anita Shreve" into the Search field and hit Enter. I see a bunch of "checks." I smile.

THINGS TO DO
WITH GINGERBREAD

upton lee

It was what we euphemistically called the holiday season. To be precise: the shopping season. And we were really intent on the gingerbread house competition. That was last year. Angela Domingo made a small gingerbread casino and Shauna made a full running mill dam.

I went traditional: a gingerbread house with a gingerbread Hansel and a gingerbread Gretel and a gingerbread witch. With a twist for the kids. They were all dinosaurs.

Then Angus Spurling came out with a gingerbread tavern. Tiny names in pinpricks on gingerbread tankards hung over the gingerbread bar. There was even a tiny drunk on a bar stool and a bartender looking irritated—which was accomplished using miniature hot cinnamons. And the entire thing was wired. With a martini sign. Which ignited. And gave out this wonderful nutmeg smell. Which seemed like cheating. He was hated, let me tell you. He got third place, though, so it was worth it.

Then Ruth constructed a Goblin's Market, but

the fruit looked like sugared meatballs, and Eunice Huang did *Vertigo* with a bell tower. She put a chalk drawing of a girl on a cobbled sidewalk with a gingerbread man half-hanging out a window high above the girl. It didn't work. Too few people had seen the movie.

What a year that was. There was a gingerbread Chartres made by Simon Illgodzenlodtz. He's dead. And so he won first place not only for the rose windows and the gargoyles but for the obvious reason that he was dead.

There was a Russian spacecraft—which was really just a crumbling house that Tinny Mort decided could be transformed into the Soyus.

Then too there was a Lincoln Monument that looked not at all like Lincoln. Our long-ago president looked like a mermaid—something about the feet. Then there was the gingerbread house that was a little more back-to-basics except it was Snow White's cottage and there were the dwarfs and there was Snow White in a spun sugar coffin. That took second place—because everyone was thinking about death last year. Again, not fair.

And so this year I say let's not think about death or—as with the Lincoln Monument—politics. My idea hasn't been done. This is it: I'm making the largest gingerbread house ever. The size of an actual house.

Maybe to be somewhat precise: it will be the size of a large tool shed.

I've been working in the garage. Ever since Sebastian moved out (I'd given him an ultimatum because I wanted children), I've been working. The garage feels vacant without Sebastian's tools hanging off the wall, and without his snowblower and the lawnmower. But the gingerbread is really taking up a lot of room, and at least I know I stuck to my principles.

The fact is: I want children. I want to make sure they're warm and fed.

Don't think I'm a witch. It's not like that. I want them thin or fat. I want to make them a home filled with warm memories. Whatever I do I don't want to hurt them. And they won't be lonely. I won't allow loneliness in my house. Loneliness is terrible.

ALEXANDERPLATZ

kyle hemmings

In the hotel room overlooking Alexanderplatz, my body spoons hers. I like to think of her flesh as a kind of honey that once flowed from the pores of ambivalent angels. It now glues me to this room. She is a German student majoring in Marketing and minoring in collecting old foreigners who still deny the existence of walls. Last night, I told her how funny it was that the Berlin Wall is now an open art gallery. Wiping a strand of hair from her face, she smirked and looked away. She now stands and lights a cigarette.

Her breasts, small and supple, remind me of apathetic birds prized for their voices, smooth as the hands of pickpockets.

Last night she told me that she has a collection of expensive watches from old boyfriends. "Are they still ticking?" I asked.

"Some still do," she said. "It's my absence that keeps them ticking."

"And your new one? The student from Munich?"

"Oh, his heart is already dead. Just the brain and

the release button are the only things that work."

My nude ballerina, who really isn't mine, performs a perfect spin.

I smile and ask when we will meet again.

"I don't know," she says. "I'm staying with a family. Maybe tomorrow for lunch in the *Kurfürstendamm*."

Lately I haven't been in the mood for McDonald's. She dresses in a plaid skirt and woolen pullover. Her legs are long and firm, shapely as a swimmer's.

"I hope the condom didn't break," she says with a wink, "if it did, I might follow you back to the States for child support. I might have a hard time explaining to this child that you are not its grandfather."

I drive her through Berlin rush-hour traffic, past the litter of fast-food wrappers, abandoned newspapers. We drive past the Brandenburg Gate. She gets out and walks over to my driver's side. A peck on the cheek. I look up at the sky, the clouds, white and grey, moving in somebody's cinematic version of slow motion.

"I wish I had a hot air balloon," I say. "I'd take you up with me and float far above Checkpoint Charlie, wave to all the tourists. Maybe we'd never come down."

She strokes my hand in light almost undetectable motions. I imagine her perfume as something shoplifted and peach-smelling mixed with the fading musk of a man's cologne.

"If I had a hot air balloon, I would go up by myself. And I would stay there forever. My own island. And if they tried to bring me down—I'd jump."

She smiles. Such a child's broad victorious smile.

"And what about me?" I ask.

"I will wave to you."

She walks away.

I listen to the metrical beat of her heels hitting cobblestone until there is no possibility of music. Above the clouds, in their flimsy lives, their free verse movements, weave past the sun, exposing a pale distant light. It must be close to three. I'm getting hungry, maybe should head towards the *Friedrichstrasse.*

I look down at my watch. It's missing.

THE OFFICE WINDOW

peter schireson

The old man avoided looking into office windows. Walking to the market, he kept to the residential side of the street, avoiding the offices on the opposite side. As December afternoons grew darker, the light coming from the office windows seemed brighter, spilling onto the sidewalk and into the street. The glow tugged at him. But he fixed his attention on the sidewalk, as though something precious and unrecoverable would leak out his eyes if he looked up.

Tonight, the office windows on the street were all dark save one. Its glow caught the corner of his eye. He paused and pictured his own office. It never had bright lighting pouring out and across a street, onto cars, onto passersby. He found brightly lit spaces uncomfortable. He liked a few small lamps. You didn't need such bright light.

The handle of his shopping bag was soft in his fingers. People walked around him. He squinted at the bright window across the street. Cars passed slowly in both directions. He waited for an opening and crossed over. He stood before the window. It was a large office, upscale in the white, antiseptic style of the day, orderly but with something amiss. The desk chair, an ergonomic construction of tubes and webbing, lay on its side on the floor. A cordless handset lay next to it. The office was otherwise unremarkable. A wide worktable faced the street. Papers and folders sat in a neat stack next to a computer monitor.

The old man was wondering why the chair and the phone were on the floor when a man walked into the office. He was Chinese, tall and handsome, about 40. His hair was fashionably cut. He wore black slacks and a white shirt, open at the neck. He had a cut on his forehead. He picked up the chair and the phone, pushed some buttons on the phone, and listened for a few seconds. He sat in the chair and wheeled himself up to the worktable. He wiggled the computer mouse and looked at the monitor. He placed his elbows on the desk and rested his face in his hands. He sat this way for nearly a minute. Then he lifted his face and ran his fingers through his hair. His eyes were closed. The old man watched without moving.

The man in the office noticed the old man and stared blankly at him for a few seconds. He glanced back at the monitor and looked back at the old man. The man in the office blinked his eyes a few times and a question seemed to form on his face for a moment, then vanish. The old man didn't move. The man in the office wheeled his chair away from the desk and stood. He walked to the side of the window and looked at the old man again. Then he reached up, and, with a long tug, pulled the curtains closed.

TEXTIQUETTE

chris henry

She hasn't answered my texts, all day. Our schedules don't really sync up too well. She's got the nine to five (which she gets up at five for), and I've got the night job at a restaurant. We've planned to meet tonight at seven, to see each other for the first time in almost a week. And she hasn't answered my texts. It's been hours.

I call. The phone rings. She doesn't answer. I leave a message. I start to get that cold feeling of panic in my stomach. It's over. Why wouldn't she call me back if she wasn't going to dump me?

Finally she texts. *Sorry, my phone was dead. Are we still on for tonight?*

Yeah fucking right your phone was dead. Dead phones go right to voicemail. But I don't say that. *Yeah, we're still on for tonight.*

I shower and get pretty. I drive over. She opens the door. Her dog still loves me.

"How was your day?"

"Oh, it was okay, what do you want to do?"

"Are you hungry? There's an Indian place around the corner, it's good."

We go. She's gorgeous, and tense, and staring at the tablecloth. I make jokes. It's barely working. But, by the time the food comes, she's starting to smile. We eat, and at her suggestion, we walk to the Whole Foods across the street to get a bottle of wine. The knot of tension in my gut starts to subside.

We get back to her apartment. I uncork the wine while she goes to the bathroom. I fill up the one wine glass she owns and hand it to her as she comes out. I go in, take a piss, wash my hands. You worry too much, I tell the mirror. Everything's fine. In an hour, we'll be kissing on the couch with wine-stained lips.

I come out of the bathroom. She is hunched over the table crying.

"What's wrong?"

"My ex just texted me that we need to talk. I'm sorry, it's just been really hard."

Ah, so that's what you've been doing all day. I wasn't being too sensitive. I was trusting my gut.

I listen to her talk about the ex. I nod and smile and take the glass of wine from her hand. I know I'm done. I'm in the process of making a polite exit. I finish the glass. She says how sorry she is for the ninth time. I give her a hug, kiss her cheeks, her forehead, her lips, then say goodnight.

My boots klonk down the apartment steps, and I push out the door onto the street. It's a cold walk back to my car. I bury my hands in my pockets, and my left hand closes around the plastic of my cell. I give it a squeeze, and a bitter giggle tweaks the corners of my mouth. I just got cock-blocked by a text.

GLASS

ellen orleans

"You have to tell them," Kevin insisted, even though you'd never imagined otherwise. You were not one to hide evidence or misdirect blame.

Besides, it was only a broken window.

Forty years later, you don't remember how it happened or what exactly broke. A storm window left leaning against the house? Or had it been that small high window in the basement? What hit it? A rock, a ball, odd matter launched from a slingshot?

You do remember a hesitation, a belief that you shouldn't get near the window because this is exactly what happens—glass breaks—and then this one did.

Your mother was angrier than you expected. A short-lived, end-of-day, not-one-more-thing anger. She said you had to tell your father when he came home from work.

You don't remember him being particularly annoyed, more of a going through the motions scolding before dinner, then, "We'll clean it up afterwards."

It must have been summer time. It was still light out.

Clothes unchanged from the office, in his dress trousers, white shirt and loosened tie, your father moved the metal frame holding the cracked glass away from the side of the house and onto the lawn. (Or had it already been there? Had you and Kevin moved the window and shattered it during transport?) Your father set down a grocery bag for the broken pieces. Or maybe he brought out that heavy paper sack from the garage, the one that had once held cement.

You crouched facing each other, picking glass from the pane, putting the pieces in the bag. Were you wearing work gloves when you did this? You can picture your hands clumsily enshrouded in them, three sizes too big. You can also picture your hands bare.

At first, your father continued to admonish. You don't remember what he told you, his chastising words, only that he stopped talking for a minute. Then he said, "But they do make such interesting shapes." He held up a rough triangle of glass, then one with points like a star, then one the shape of Montana. "Aren't they almost beautiful?"

You were not prepared for any of it. Not the early end to the lecture. Not the switch in topics. Certainly not the thoughtfulness. His softness.

"Why are they all so different?" you asked, reaching into the grass for another piece, long and slender this time, dropping it into the bag.

"I don't know," he said, again surprising you. No lesson on the molecular composition of glass or covalent bonding. "This one is nearly round."

And in this way, the two of you continued your harvest, marvelling quietly at the random, lovely shapes—their shadows long and indistinct on the plush summer lawn.

DEPARTED

kerry workman

In all my smallness I stand beside her, my head back, looking up under her arm, seeing the soft loose white skin of her arm dangling as she works at the stove. I hear the sizzle and smell the tortilla she presses on the skillet. She murmurs something to me and looks down, her smile is an ocean. My father comes and stands in the doorway and I am happy because she is too and he lifts me and thrills me, throwing me high.

I grow bigger and the world becomes night when the walls shudder and his voice rolls like a truck through the house and I try to make myself invisible in my bed while my mother yells and cries. She tells me on a cold morning that she called the cops and my father was departed to Mexico. I ask her when will he come home? Never, she says. You never come back after you are departed. At the Iglesia de la Inmaculada Concepcion we sit on hard shiny benches, the roof of the church as high as heaven. We are up close to the altar, where I can see Jesus hanging on the cross, the blood dripping from his head, his hair long and stuck to his cheeks. The Virgin Mary stands in the corner in a flowing blue robe edged in gold that covers her head, and drapes over her shoulders and breasts, and she looks down by her feet with great sadness. My mother tells me to pray. She tells me to pray that she is not departed. I hold her hand and we walk silently over to the Holy Virgin Mother and light two candles and I pray with my lips moving that I may keep my mother. I pray that my sins will be washed clean and that my forgiveness will buy me my mother, because unlike me she was not born in San Antonio and so she does not have eternal life. I am blessed because I was born in San Antonio. My mother has told me this many times. But I don't think I want eternal life if my father and my mother are both departed. I ask my mother if I can depart with her and she cries and says no, children do not belong in Mexico, it is not a good place for them.

When the padre blesses me taking communion he says, "Suffer the little children to come unto me," and I keep my head down, trying to wipe my eyes and my nose without anyone seeing me, because I am afraid of Mexico, but I am more afraid of eternal life without my mother.

CONVICTION

angela rydell

Sweating despite the air-conditioning, Selma adds a hammer to her burgeoning cart. Not to hurt anyone, break into anything. Not anymore. Just fixing her apartment window.

She's reformed. But everyone stares as if she still wore an orange jump suit that shouted: "Convicted felon, mugger." As if the cart she pushes were a cage she'd best be locked inside.

The loudspeaker crackles that special again. Static scrapes like sandpaper.

Gasps, even groans surround her. People scramble, search their carts, each other's, gape at hers. Two teenage boys, their carts mounded like anthills, cuss as she walks by.

"*You're* the one," an old man frowns.

Selma hurries past, head down.

"It's her."

One woman, her cart filled with a lifetime supply of Tide detergent, smiles. Does she know? Selma's finally good? "They want you in the back office," she says. "It's you! Four twenty-eight, see!" She points to the number at the head of Selma's cart.

Selma's stomach turns to ice. Who is this woman? Who are *they*?

The loudspeaker, static-free at last, announces, "Will the customer with cart 428 please go to the service desk in the back of the store."

The old anger rises between her shoulder blades, up her neck, constraining her throat. Dr. Stevens counseled her about this. "It may seem like people are staring, thinking only about you, that everything they say is about you. That's just the paranoia. They can't read your mind."

A blue-haired woman walks by, whispers, "Take something expensive! This is your chance!"

Just paranoia? Dr. Stevens was wrong. Dead wrong.

Anger fills her teeth. She tries to reach for the hammer in her cart without looking suspicious. Selma's good at trying not to look suspicious.

Feet shuffling as if chained together, Selma pushes toward the back where a man behind a counter watches, grins, offers his hand. Selma tightens her grip on her hammer, looks beyond him to the dark, confining rooms in the back. This is where they think she belongs?

She won't go back there. Lets her face go blank, her whole body drain—except for the anger, the weight of her hammer.

People crowd behind her. Breathe down her neck. One little boy practically crawls into her cart. "Cool!" he yells, poking her Nintendo.

She wants to slam him away.

"Doesn't happen every day, does it?" The man sees her hand clench and unclench in a fist, steps back. "Everything in your whole cart. Free!"

The word enters her, moves like a breeze through her tight shoulders, loosens her knuckles, fills the blankness of her mind.

"Me?" she breathes. "Free?"

SCHOLASTIC APTITUDE TEST

tom hazuka

"If a baker's dozen is thirteen, what's eleven? A faker's dozen?"

I smile across the table at my blind date, figuring that's the expected reward for her cleverness. She's reacting to my comment about *Cheaper by the Dozen*, how insane it must be dealing with so many kids. But instead I see that she's serious. Dead serious. She's on the verge of tears. I'm on the verge of deciding to throttle my sister Gail for setting me up with her fellow seventh grade teacher. Irene was "intriguing," said Gail's letters to me in Vietnam. Irene saw the world the way I did, "just off-kilter enough to make it interesting."

But off-kilter is the last thing I find interesting these days, so I stop pretending that my ex-wife is a blind date. That date happened over twenty years ago, the summer of the Watergate hearings, the summer I came home from the war. The Supreme Court had just decided Roe v. Wade. My date's soft (not that I had confirmed yet that it was soft, but I knew) almond hair hung almost to her beaded belt.

She wore turquoise earrings and an attitude foreign to any teacher I'd ever had, even in college. What my sister called "off-kilter," I called wonderful.

"If I made up the SAT, man," Irene said, "I'd ask relevant questions. Ones with answers like 'The Pope is to birth control as Nixon is to Vietnam.'"

We were halfway through our second Singapore Sling, and this comment seemed a revelation. This woman seemed like my answer. When we revealed that we both got 1350 on the SAT, it seemed like a sign.

Now, halfway through our glasses of mineral water, we are deciding like rational adults how often I should see my two children, who after all have a stepfather who loves them and has feelings too. I think of the fetuses, one aborted, one miscarried, who would have been our children instead, because never did we plan on more than two.

My ex-wife looks strange with hair shorter than mine. She notices me noticing.

"I felt like I needed a change." She fluffs it up in back. "What do you think?"

"I know what you mean."

"That doesn't answer the question."

There's a catch in her throat. I cough to try and clear mine.

"Unless you can eliminate some of the wrong answers," I say to the wall above her shoulder, "you're better off leaving it blank."

PHASES

william r. stoddart

Jack sat on a lawn chair above the floodwall that kept the mountain stream from the cabin. The sound of the water helped him to relax. He ate just enough to stay alive, and the little he ate made him feel uncomfortably full. He hadn't eaten since yesterday evening, and it was time for "phase one" which was his euphemism for before dinner drinks.

"I'll have the merlot."

Jack's wife was there to make his drinks, administer his drugs and listen when he got to the talkative parts during phase three.

"Wine glass or water?" Jack's wife, Susan, asked.

"Wine glass. We may be camping, but let's not lose our dignity," Jack spoke, barely audibly above the sound of the stream.

Jack's stomach cancer was in remission. His leukemia was in the acute stage. Susan delivered the merlot to Jack and opened another lawn chair beside him.

"You need to eat something," Susan said.

"Not hungry. Thirsty. Phase one in progress."

Jack spoke that way on purpose. It pissed off Susan. He was typically mean during phase one.

"If you pass out I can't carry you into the cabin, and that nice park ranger goes home at five o'clock. You'll spend the night out here and freeze." Susan was matter-of-fact with Jack because he was dying.

Jack was on his procrit cycle and had energy for the camping trip. The drug gave him a boost of red blood cells, which was a false thing, as everyone knew the bad white cells would eventually win. "They always win out," his doctor had assured him, "and it will kill you sure, but you got some living to do for awhile."

Jack talked about beer during phase one. He loved to drink beer before he developed stomach cancer.

"I loved the cheap, ice cold, light beer. I could drink gallons on a hot day." Jack's reminiscing was the prelude to phase two, which was the transition from wine to bourbon whiskey.

"I'd like to die sitting here," Jack said flatly.

"That would be just like you. The funeral home is one hundred miles west of here. That would be inconvenient for everyone. I might just let the bears eat you." Susan didn't bother to look into Jack's eyes any more when she spoke to him.

The wind blew through the trees and sounded like the rush of water. Susan walked into the cabin to get warm.

BE KIND

linh dinh

Seeing him sitting alone, hard up as usual, she gave him a tight, sustained hug. With a brief giggle, she actually said, "I think you need this." It's not costing me anything, she thought. My softness is appeasing his anger, his rage at not being laid for, I don't know, many months now.

She wasn't in the least attracted to him, so this act was pure charity. More people should do this, she thought, give hard up acquaintances much needed physical contact. It will cost you nothing, and you will make someone feel wanted, if only for a moment. My softness against his hard upness—how beautiful and vivid is the English language, how accurate—is much appreciated, I'm sure, she continued to think, as she felt, however briefly, his hard on.

How sad it is to wander around for hours with an overheated and neglected bodily conjunction, protuberance or crevice, as you eye and nearly rub against bodies that whisper or scream, entwine with me, my dear, but none of it is meant for you.

At home, later, she thought that her brief attention was rather condescending. Maybe he didn't appreciate my kind gesture, my pity, but resented it. She also thought that she was being rather niggardly. Why stop at a hug? Though he was so hard up, he would probably hug anything, even a cabbage, it was obvious that he would rather have skin against skin, not several layers of clothes causing minor friction. It wouldn't have cost her anything to say, Hey, let's go to my place. In fact, she lived right on the next block. Let's go to my place, she should have said with a smile and a brief giggle.

As stated, she wasn't the least bit attracted to him. Without going into details, let's say he was sexually neutral. Some people are like that. Where heat and even madness should issue, there's only a microwave oven, so to speak, and a broken one.

It would be so sad, their love making, and so beautiful, since no one is more naked than when he's absolutely desperate. A pitiably starving man is kind of a sexual turn on, she entertained. I might just cry before, during and after.

JERRY'S TV

brian alan ellis

Jerry's TV was stolen. I suspect his estranged wife of taking it. If you ask me, Jerry got off easy. My ex-wife took the kids. But this isn't about me, it's about Jerry. And now that his TV is gone and he can't watch *Lost*, well, he's all tore up inside.

All day I hear Jerry pacing. Through the ceiling of my apartment I hear it. I hear his slippers shuffling back and forth, back and forth. Those damn slippers. Sometimes, at night, I can hear him sobbing a little. He snores too, but he was doing that even when he had a TV.

I mean, it's not like he has the money to get another one; his wife must've taken that, too. In fact, I'm surprised the poor bastard still has a roof over his head—hell, with all that floorboard-walking he does, I'm surprised *I* still have one. Roofs aren't cheap. Cob, our landlord, doesn't care. Poor Jerry could fall right through the floor into my apartment, breaking both legs, and Cob still wouldn't do shit. That's how Cob is.

It sounds insane, but I considered having Jerry

over at my place. Then I remembered: I don't have cable. In fact, I don't even own a TV. And even if I did have cable and a TV I'd still be wary of having Jerry over. For starters, he's messy—watching the man eat Ritz crackers will attest to that. Secondly, and for obvious reasons, I wouldn't want that estranged wife of his, old sticky fingers, to know where I live. As for *Lost*, well, I'd already seen it—when it was called *Gilligan's Island.*

Regardless, the season finale is only a week away, and still no TV for Jerry—just the threat of my ceiling caving in, just a grown man sobbing. It's a real shame. But you can't say I didn't try. I did.

The other day I went door to door asking all the neighbors to pitch in to help buy Jerry a new TV, but all I got was $2.63 and a lifetime of poor excuses. So to spare Jerry the embarrassment of knowing he has cheap neighbors, I put the money towards buying myself a pack of smokes. Kools. As for the lifetime of poor excuses, well, there isn't much you can do about that.

CIVILIAN WAR DREAM

jamey trotter

It was a draft of sorts. Someone from the government, a woman, knocked on my suburban door. She asked if I was ready to go. I was. I picked up my bag. You won't be needing that. I kissed the downy head of my daughter. My wife wished me a good trip. She didn't know; none of us knew.

I was loaded into a van with some other men. They were my best friends, but I didn't know them. We were en route. Commercial airplanes were crashing all around us. The enemy drove them, first a commuter plane into a department store, then a small jet into an office building. Then a big jet into the ocean. So horrific, so original. I cried. I was scared.

The Taliban had a prison somewhere in Africa. We were there. I saw what was going on. "How can I be a prisoner? I'm not even a soldier. I don't even know how to escape prison if I get the chance. I don't even know how to fire a gun."

The government woman responded while another plane went down behind her in the background: "It doesn't matter. The Taliban wants an equal number of prisoners before they will sign the peace treaty. You and your buddies have too much credit card debt to ever recover; this way, that gets wiped clean when you get out. In the meantime, you are a hero to your country. Thank you, sir."

I was hyperventilating. An American was wheeled out from the doors of the prison. He had a shirt on, and boots. His entire groin area was duct-taped. "They don't let you shit, man."

As I entered, the prison was like third-world prisons you imagine when you imagine them, dark and rank with mean looking men running them. I wanted to shit so bad, but I didn't have to go. Through a window, another plane crashed into the ground. I could hear the screams of the passengers before impact. A few more prisoners and this would stop. I was allowed a bowel movement in a relatively clean bathroom before we were told to go in, my buddies and me.

We were the last few.

SOMEWHERE JUST OUTSIDE OF FRESNO CLOWNS ARE BUILDING HOUSES OUT OF CHEESEBURGERS

jon olsen

Nothing is known about the clowns, who they are, where they come from, or how they ended up living out there in that baking wasteland of exploded tires and incinerated trailers. They can only be glimpsed from a distance, mirage-like, from the shoulder of the freeway.

There is a hillock behind some dumpsters in back of the Shell station off Exit ____, and you can climb to the top of this mound of dirt, sculpted by long extinct earth moving machines, and toss cheeseburgers down the steep slope on its backside. The slope is very steep, and no one, not even the cockiest, drunkest teenaged jackass, dares to try and climb down it. The terrain below is a graveyard of jagged metal rusting in pools of putrid tar. And far beyond this festering death zone, faintly moving back and forth in the distance, just shy of the horizon, are the clowns.

The traffic passing through here has ballooned steadily over the past six years. An insanely long parade of cars crawls by the drive-thru window of the nearby Burger King, which now sells specially prepared value packs of "Clown Whoppers," something like six bucks for a bag of eight. The tourists carry these bulging, dripping grease bags up the hillock and hurl them as far out as they're able, and then squint into the distance to see if the clowns react. The clowns never react. They seem oblivious to the world outside of their wasteland. But every morning, all the cheeseburgers that have been thrown over the slope are gone. And with a good pair of binoculars or a camcorder zoom lens, it is just possible to see the mounds of accumulated cheeseburgers and the never-ending toil of the clowns, building their odd, sagging, dripping houses.

To people who grew up around here, the crowds of tourists are almost as baffling as the clowns. We collect the tourists' money, and we watch them drive through our service stations, wondering how long it will take for the growing stench of rotting meat to finally drive them away.

FUN HOUSE

robert scotellaro

She'd gotten the fun house mirrors at an auction and had them put up in the spare bedroom. He found them strange, even a little disturbing, and thought the buy extravagant with the kids away at college and the big tuition bucks spilling out. But she'd insisted on a "well deserved splurge" after all that straight and narrow. A side of her, new to him.

So he went along. Even following her one night, with a bottle of Marqués de Riscal, into that room with the lights dimmed and candles she placed on both dressers, adding to the mix. In bed, she began taking off her clothes, then his. "No way," he said, draining the last of the wine, gazing into one of the mirrors overhead, at their stretched-out, undulating forms—fleshy waves of them in the sheets.

He started to sit up, but she pulled him back. "This is weird, Connie," he said.

She reached out a zigzaggy hand and ran it down his zigzaggy middle. Looking left, she was squat and condensed, her cheeks bulged as if she had two apples stuffed in her mouth—her breasts large, wobbly globes. She guided his hand to them.

In another, the two of them were amoeboid, transforming silvery strangers. "You've got to be kidding me," he said. She smiled. And at a glance it was an astonishingly wide curl, liquid as mercury. He continued shifting his vision.

"My God!" he said.

"What?"

"The size of that thing."

She leaned over and whispered something. A name, he thought—not his own. Perhaps an endearment. She shook out her hair—jagged bolts against his chest. He closed his eyes, and when he opened them she was wriggly and rosy. A stick figure, a block, a fleshy smear—strange and elegant. He heard some low, guttural sounds—his own.

She bit his shoulder and he pulled her close. His eyes banged against each corner of their sockets. The room was cluttered. It was ablaze with candlelight— squat fiery balls, elongated licks of light, and all their odd and flagrant infidelities in every piece of glass.

A PHOTO

matthew rafferty

The flash caught me staring out the window; both sides of my Beatles bowl haircut are visible. I was wearing a plaid shirt, my mother always dressed me in plaid. She says she knew it was cool in 1982, the rest of the world had to wait for Eddie Bauer to tell them. In my hand is a wooden building block with a red letter 'A' on the reflection's side; 'A' is for Apostate.

I was four years old, and the expression on my face knows nothing of disfellowshipping. I was unaware that a mother could cross the street to ignore her son, or turn the warmth of a smile into twisted lips. I was simply happy to be away from home, staying in a hotel, just returned from the daylong insemination at the annual Convention of Jehovah's Witnesses. 'A' is for Amen, Brother.

Oklahoma City sidewalks show beyond the window. Men in suits wearing "Brother ____" name badges wave their arms in too-long arcs as they walk before their women and children. Caught in the flash are their expressions as they look at the worldly around them: disdain, an abacus accounting of "What do I get when Jehovah kills all these people?" The children look to their fathers with the same look mirrored on my face. Eyes brimming with joy at the secret we share. 'A' is for Annihilation.

I wonder now at that little boy so full of promise, so eager to please. My mother stood behind me with the camera staring at the back of my head. Even as a boy there must have been some sign that I was flawed. I was not like the others. I was too smart. I evidenced an unwashable core of sound reasoning. I wore my clip-on tie slightly off-center. Mother must have known when she looked at my face in the glass, when she saw the 'A' held in my tiny hands. 'A' is for Alone.

LIFE AND MEDICINE

bill rector

Lecture I

I have been a physician longer than most of you students have been alive. How distant the future must seem. How eager you must be for it to arrive! How much more this gray head must seem to hold than yours. Young friends, nascent colleagues, caretakers of my own advancing years, I confess that I have forgotten nearly all I once knew. I have passed so far beyond Introductory Physics that I approach weightlessness. I have spun the objective of Beginning Biology so far beyond the highest power that I now find myself returning my own gaze. I have gone farther. I have passed multiple choice tests in which no answer is true and have done so with perfect scores. I have done this again and again. You will, too. You will do everything I say. It will happen before you know it. Gray rain of the ceiling, white dew on the desk.

Lecture II

Remember how, like astringent tears, formalin burned your eyes at first? You thought you'd never see your way through. But you learned. You learned names—the body seemed composed of nothing else—stringy tendons in the wrist, the shattered plate of bones that make up the hand, interminable lists of nerves. It seemed more than one could retain, but you learned to adapt, accept without blinking what you were taught were "the facts." In your second year the hospital replaced the lab. The simple alphabet of the ECG clearly spelled *Atrial Flutter* or *Heart Attack*, CT scans' green marquees announced *Metastatic Cancer* or *Liver Abscess,* and routine blood tests returned in bold or red that even the dullest could repeat on rounds: *Abnormal, Alert!*

Now, ready to graduate and take the oath, you send messages across the room on the stubby wings of your highly trained thumbs. *Why can't he be clear? What point is he trying to make in the final lecture of the year?*

AFTER THE FUNERAL: DUBLIN, 1960

mark fallon

The priest is in the parlor with the Aunties.

"Have a biscuit with that, Father?"

Peg offers him the plate, swipes at me when I go for one.

"Let him alone, can't you?" says Maureen. "On this of all days."

Then they're at it, tearing strips off one another. Nothing new.

Red-faced, wrinkled and dusted with cigarette ash, the priest is sinking into the armchair, a bottle of Hennessy within easy reach.

Outside the rain has stopped long enough for the older men to smoke Woodbines in the yard and talk through rotted teeth. "What in the name of god is he wearing now?" says Uncle Paddy, making a drunken grab at me. When I tell him it's a pocket square he bursts out laughing, like he always does. Dad just gozzies on the cement, rubs it in with a polished boot, gives me his back.

Upstairs the bedroom curtains are drawn and Mam is laid out in her Sunday best under the warm glow of the bedside lamp. From the sound of it the crowd below is getting rowdy, so I close the door and switch on the gramophone. The needle crackles in the grooves.

Carefully, I unwind a rosary someone has placed in Ma's cold hands and get rid of it, as she has made me swear to do.

I take the hairbrush from the dresser and bring it through her long brown hair. There we are on the bed, the two of us, with John McCormack in the background singing "Macushla."

I check myself in the mirror, adjusting my pocket square, which I spied in a copy of my Mam's *Vogue* and which was a silk. Blue. Cerulean. I am nine years old and I know this. My version is a folded piece of tea towel I thought had an interesting pattern.

WHAT WERE YOU THINKING?

mark fallon

You're standing in sweltering heat on the outer ledge of a bridge in one of those Pacific Rim countries where there are earthquakes. As soon as the tiny man next to you gives the signal, you're going to bungee-jump 400 feet into the gorge below.

It's all part of the same thing.

Last summer, your forty-third, you were diagnosed HIV positive.

"It's not a death sentence anymore," said your best friend.

You bleached your hair and got a Mohawk.

Six months ago it was a ring through your left nipple. Then you started in on your ears. In fact, by the time you get back Stateside the earrings you've ordered—chrome rivets just like you saw on that hot guy in the subway—should have arrived.

At a queer bar in the red-light district last night you got talking with a trio of twenty-somethings from back home. One of them had a bar code tattooed on the nape of his neck (already you're making plans to get inked). The talk ranged from marriage equality to that singer who's fucking that film star, until it was late and conversation turned to today. They were making plans to bus about an hour north to go bungee-jumping: Are you interested?

The others are on the ground far below. You can hear their hoots although you cannot see them. You watched them, one by one, lean out into air, plummet with accelerating force only to be denied, at the last moment, by the elastic cord snaking their ankles.

You're suddenly hit by an overwhelming wave of terror. And it isn't about the jump. "You go now," says the tiny man, giving you the thumbs up. He ignores your middle-aged Mohawk, is oblivious to your western existential bullshit. He beams up at you from a face that conceals no motive.

THE MUSTACHE HE'S ALWAYS WANTED BUT COULD NEVER GROW

brian alan ellis

They will lie in bed, the two of them, their sweaty, naked flesh suctioned together as they rest on their sides—him facing the back of her body, she the wall. The strands of her dark hair hanging under his nose, like the moustache he's always wanted but could never grow, will remind him of a warm, bubbly bath. And as she hums the melody of a song he cannot place, he will try forcing an erection between her ass cheeks. She will of course refuse this invasion by elbowing him in the chest, and he will wonder aloud what the difference between putting something in one place and not the other is. Then she will ask, in so many words, why he hates women so much. This question will befuddle him, and he will tell her, in so many words, that when it comes to the attainment of absolute beauty there can never be any hatred involved. And before she can take in such a response he will tickle her, and she will laugh while her legs kick the sheets off the bed. And as she goes to retrieve the sheets she has kicked off the bed while laughing, he will put all beauty on its belly and slide it in, keeping it, reaching, while her cat sitting at the corner of the bed, its head titled at a confused angle, looks on. When he finishes he will roll off of her, and he will grin while lighting a cigarette. He won't ask her if she came or not; he didn't ask the first time. Then he will stuff his hand inside a Kleenex box. It will be empty, and he will use a sock instead.

IT'S ABOUT THE LOONS

charles rutter

I stare into a star-wept sky, and fill myself with the gin and tonic flavor of fallen needles. My neck glows firelight orange as father prepares fish.

The scent of pine needles sings from the ground, the odor of needles whirls, cascading up in a shower of smells.

The scent of pine needles seems everywhere, and the musky, dust-odor of untrampled dirt. Somewhere north of the Falls, Father fills a bowl with...

My father crouches near the fire and pours beer into a mix of dry batter. He hands me a can and a quiet wink. "Don't tell your mother" that words can't build a memory.

After dinner, the loons begin to sing, and my father ululates.

He repeats loon songs in Hepburn's shaky warble, "Norman, the loons are singing."

How many times did he sit and myna back the line a curmudgeon spoke to a dentist? "Ethel Thayer. Sounds like I'm lisping." How many times did he watch his mother's dust-ordered brain forget his name, and Norman forget his in a picture frame? "Who the hell is that? Who's in this picture here?" He was always fond of Fonda.

How many times?

That movie, he said, was about death, and daughters, and fathers, and loons. And dentists, and aging, and puzzles, and fishing. It was about picking strawberries when you can't find your way home.

Once, when I was still young, a black bear came to camp with us. A hatchet flew from my father and clanged loud and awkward at the bear's feet. He ran in fear, as did my father, who bear-hugged our five-man tent staked tight to the ground and ripped it from its plot in a single easy heave. We never went back for the hatchet.

DUST TO DUST

nick kimbro

The plastic jack-o-lantern rests on its side, propped against a tombstone and grinning into the ground. Candy is pooled around it in the dirt, and she lies nearby on a damp plot of earth where the ground was struck but the grave never dug. The boys search for her among the stones.

Yoohoo. Come out wherever you are.

She closes her eyes and rocks from side to side, upending the dirt with her shoulders and shifting deeper with each movement. Worms writhe on top of her as the clumps of dirt break apart: centipedes, beetles, and slugs. The boys still are calling and she tries to remain still. A spider crawls along her forearm, eight points of contact. Her hairs stand on end. She can feel each of its legs on her skin—not quite a caress—and the beetles burrow in between her and the ground. Worms twist like curled leaves in the wind.

Her senses rise into her pores, like an electric current on top of water. Her body is a city, a sanctuary, giving shelter to the insects whispering into her flesh, filling it with a language none but her can understand.

Where are you, sweetheart? I just want a treat.

Her fingers clutch at the earth by her sides. She feels along each slope and between her legs, at last grasps a pine cone and holds it against the seam of her pants. It pricks her hands. She twists the pine cone against her like a pestle—she is the mortar—and can feel her ashes mixing with the mud. The boys' voices recede while she grinds it against her. Her mouth is open. She is sand. She is sugar. She disappears.

LEOPARD-SKIN HAT

jo cannon

She wondered if the strip of blotched tatty fur around his hat was real leopard skin. His knuckles on the steering wheel were fuzzy blond; his thighs, thick in tight shorts, spread wide on the sticky leather of the bakkie.

"I don't know how you stand it, working with them all day," he said.

"People are people," she said.

He was silent, trying hard. Susan was aware of her breath leaking into the dusty heat between them, his sharp sweat. When he'd invited her to the farm for the weekend there seemed no polite way to refuse. She could hardly fake a prior engagement in this town where nothing happened and every conversation was observed. When the bakkie called for her that morning the kids swarmed, delighted at two mzungus together: a matching pair. She felt compromised just climbing into the passenger seat beside the manager from the tobacco estate.

She wound down the window, but even the air outside was stifling. As they passed a village, a woman sweeping the dirt outside her thatched hut waved. Dirk braked hard and swore when a line of little pigs ran across the road.

"Sorry," he said.

The landscape was sea-flat, the occasional tree stripped like a mast. Tiny farmed patches of maize gave way to dry grass that bent wearily beneath the high white sky.

"I love this drive. The sky is so big here," Dirk said.

He started to sing in a strong clear tenor, about love and home and longing. She felt a rush in her belly. The road ahead was unknowable and astonishing, and for a moment the heat held them both in its palm.

MOTHER'S LAST WISHES

sarah russell

Dear Children,

These are my final requests:

Jeff, since the accident of your impending birth led to my marrying your father, I am putting you in charge of parceling out what is left of the estate. Try to be more fair to your siblings than your father was to me.

Susan, you have always been good at arranging things, like that abortion you never told me about, so you are in charge of my cremation. I have no intention of lying next to that man in a burial plot like I had to for thirty-eight years—or alone in a urn for that matter. Let my ashes find a bit of freedom in the wind. You should understand as you have chosen freedom over giving me grandchildren.

Jack—Jackson, you have always been my favorite, you know. But although I told you that you were named for a great uncle, that is not the case. In Morristown, you will find a Jackson Tulley listed in the phonebook. He has waited thirty-two years to meet you.

Regarding my funeral, go to no more trouble than you did when you sent me to hospice rather than taking me into one of your homes. No maudlin songs or scripture. Just say I was a woman to whom life dealt a pair of deuces in a high-stakes game, and that I bluffed as best I could.

Advice? Don't settle. It will devour you.

As ever,
   Mother

SEDUCTION OF AN OBLATE SPHEROID

jo cannon

"I need to talk to you about oblate spheroids," he said.

At first he was hesitant, watching her face. Then became animated as he spoke of his feelings for certain arithmetic shapes, boasted of past triumphs and hinted at future adventures. Sketching air geometry with his fork, his eyes were opaque.

"Why are you telling me this?" she asked.

His pupils refocused. "I thought you should know, if we're to carry on seeing each other. You seem the sort of woman who—"

"Who what?" she said, sharply.

"If it's too complex, I'd rather you said so now," he replied.

"Look, I think you should know straight off. I could never oblate. The idea is distasteful. Not that I've even considered it before."

He studied her. "Oblate, no. But spheroid... well, don't count it out."

There entered her head, unbidden, an image of her aspect ratio. He smiled as if he could see it too.

She felt naked, manipulated and somehow spherical.

"You are the most perfectly spheroid woman," he whispered. "But not a prolate one, oh no! Come back to my place and rotate around my minor axis. You and me, girl, together we'll make beautiful ellipsoids."

Suddenly she realised why her relationships foundered. At some level she'd always known her polar axis was shorter than her equatorial circle. She took his hand and smiled. It wasn't the candlelight or wine. At last she'd met her rotationally symmetric man.

TOOTHPICK CHURCHES

stace budzko

Near the end of things he started building a replica of The Cathedral of the Immaculate Conception with toothpicks and glue. Not only was this the church where he was baptized and served as altar boy, but here was where he shared wedding vows with his first and only true love. So familiar was he with its neo-Gothic architecture, he could make to scale the vaulted ceilings and main aisle without a ruler. So precise were the angles of each diminutive fitting, it could house the faithful comfortably (even with the imposing pillars on each side of the nave that formed those impressive arches). And this was only the inside. More remarkable was how he showcased the steeples—their highest point skyward and threatening, overlooking Casco Bay—ready to scratch the heavens. A celestial celebration, that hobby structure. How it hit the eye as the very wonder of flight itself. Is there any doubt such forms go unnoticed in the most obvious light? Sadly, yes. He knew it all too well. And what were those ends of things *things* exactly?

If I told you marriage and family would that make a lick of difference? If I told you his wife would eventually toss the model out the window does it change your thoughts on love? Piece by everlasting piece, we act like we never kiss, pretend we never meet. As much as we try, we try some more.

THE PROMISE OF
LEGO BUILDERS

sophie rosenblum

I chew my spoon, replaying untied states, the mistakes of a dyslexic, the break in convenience of textbook answers. My daydreams are smudged with capital Es as threes and miles and miles of sand for dessert. Wednesdays in February, even the date lacks permanence. The school cafeteria Mac & Cheese sits tacky and yellow like my Boxer's vomit the day he found the sponges beneath my mother's sink.

Dinner at home, away from the tinted red cup, I ask again how someone who is "good at Legos" will ever achieve anything.

My father says, "Listen."

My father says, "Stop."

He says, "Picasso, Einstein, Muhammad Ali."

I scream, "I wish I'd never taught you anything!"

We don't go back and forth like a seesaw, I simply squeeze down the slide. When I am rude, I bring flowers. Hydrangeas by the handful.

He says, "Get yourself a hobby."

I say, "Get yourself a wife."

When Cheryl left, I found a note wrapped in pink tissue paper behind my father's razor. In handwriting crisp and even as a math book, she'd written, *It takes a brave man to raise a special child.*

"What's so special about me?" I asked. "And what's so brave about you?"

BUKOWSKI

faye kicknosway

Bukowski was a twelve-year-old girl from Roanoke, Virginia, who had never been to the circus and wore white socks that were always eaten down to her instep by her always too big ugly brown shoes.

Her mother rag curled her hair and dreamed of orange juice and 1943.

Bukowski was a virgin and thought sex had something to do with eating too much spaghetti and throwing up.

Bukowski could almost tell you where California is.

Peter Max borrowed Mary Baker Eddy's telephone to ask Bukowski if he could have a Polaroid of her left ear lobe. Libra rising had something to do with it.

Bukowski liked birds and cement. She was partial to celery, coffee, and living on the third floor.

There was a man the size of a belly button in the middle of Bukowski's forehead who winked her awake.

Bukowski always put her left shoe on first because she was practicing to be Fred Astaire.

Bukowski thought L.A. meant left angles, not Los Angeles.

Bukowski's heart was not made of long, sharp, pointy fangs the way she bragged it was; instead, it was more like a wimpy, infected little toe.

OUT OF PLACE

kristine ong muslim

Never mind the draft seeping between the floorboards. The beast is already awake, and you are late for work again. You are now snagged between the juggernaut's front teeth. The snooze button of the alarm clock, a whining sound that used to be a scream back when you were nimble and hard to please.

The train breezed past you. The man behind the sliding door gave you the finger when the glass doors slid shut with the finality of a hydraulic hiss.

The man inside the elevator winked at you, closing the doors in your face as you scampered to catch that slit of hope, that receding gap between the elevator doors. If you can only squeeze yourself in, glide along the corridors straight to your cubicle where the unaccomplished city of your corporate daydreams sprawls fully booked and tampered, then nobody will ever notice that you are late again for the fourth time this month.

Somewhere, a postcard is folded against the grain. You ache with your remaining left hand, and you snap with your fist. That déjà vu buzzing. That disconnect happening once again.

WAITING FOR NOTHING

rupan malakin

Beyond the airplane window, sunset smeared the sky pus yellow, mucus yellow, the yellow of dying skin. He tried to forget the empty seat beside him, the tired smile she gave when he said he would be back that evening, the knowledge of himself as less than the man he wanted to be: a man noble, forced to act by principle, as if choice were a matter of circumstance. What else could he have done? Share cheese and wine on a hospital bed? Stare forever at the things she had touched—pencils, cutlery, her soiled underwear in the laundry basket? Was he to fish her rotting tissues from the bin and clutch them to his chest? Wait to share tears and guilt and gratitude at some trite ceremony? He had never been that man.

Florida will be warm this time of year, the limbo between summer and winter. He will rent a small room in Miami, close to the beach. He will be found lying beneath the insipid sun, reading a copy of *Crime and Punishment* made of blank pages, counting the seconds, waiting for nothing.

WOLF BLITZER

andrew bales

An unfortunate sight, Wolf Blitzer as a child. Like a bobble-head doll cast into the real world. He was never meant to be a child. His hair already graying, crow's feet pulling at his eyes. The boys on the playground circle him and press him for that heroic story his name demands. There must be a legend in there. Wolf Blitzer. Just say it.

He never asked for the name, his grandfather's. Never asked his dad to fit him with those wire-framed glasses, his mom to lick the comb and swoop his hair just so. Never asked for that suit filled out with thick shoulder pads. Never asked to be put on the spot. Never asked to be prepped and patted on the back and set out towards failure.

Tonight on CNN, in *The Situation Room*, I can see it in his dreary eyes. He's lost in a prompter, rattling off something banal. He's overcast, hidden among graphic screens, an expansive set, his own name in flashing red letters.

ASHES

albert garcía elena
(translated from spanish by kona morris)

I recall the day that, in kindergarten, we made a clay ashtray for Father's Day. With a toothpick I wrote the name of mine, Vincent. When I handed it to him, he told me he didn't smoke, gave me a condescending pat on my shoulder, and tossed it in the trash.

I remember all of this as I throw the cremation box into the first garbage bin I see after leaving the funeral home. I don't smoke either.

BUM

eric higgins

I spent my first full day after getting out of jail in the park. Next to the shrubs, they and I shook. Across my knees came and went the muzzles of dogs—some stray, some chained. But all day to people I appeared quiet.